MW01247687

Reprogramming
Carlos

JR THOMPSON

JR THOMPSON

REPROGRAMMING
CARLOS

WORTHY BATTLE SERIES BOOK 3

Other Books By JR Thompson

Harmony Series
Hidden in Harmony: Danger is Imminent
Fighting for Farmington: Destruction is Inevitable
Terrors of Troy: Despair is Inflicted
Storms at Shelton: Deception is Inexcusable

Standalones:
Revenge Fires Back
Shady Valentine
Snowflakes To Iron (ebook only)

Worthy Battle Series:
Rebuilding Alden
Redirecting Billy
Reprogramming Carlos
Reforming Dawson
Renovating Elliot
Refurbishing Felipe (coming 2019)

This is a work of fiction. Names, characters, businesses, places, events, locations, and incidents are either the products of the author's imagination or used in a fictitious manner. Any resemblance to actual persons, living or dead, or actual events is purely coincidental.

Cover design by JR Thompson.

Discover more about Christian Author JR Thompson and his writings at www.jrthompsonbooks.com

All scriptures quoted and referenced in this book are taken from the Authorized King James Bible.

Copyright 2018 JR Thompson

All rights reserved. No portion of this book may be reproduced, stored in a retrieval system, or transmitted in any form or by any means—electronic, mechanical, photocopy, recording, scanning, or other—except for brief quotations in critical reviews or articles, without the prior permission of the author.

ISBN-13: 978-1-7337673-1-6

I am dedicating this book to Hunter Handy, a young man I had the privilege of leading to the Lord in the summer of 2017. I have witnessed God doing great things in his life already and can't wait to see what He has in store for Hunter's future.

1

Captain Carlos — the name had an authoritative ring to it. Yes, that's how the thirteen-year-old would introduce himself to the overwhelming flood of reporters. When their vehicles raced up, he would strut outside in his award-winning superhero costume — the one which had earned him an incredible five-day vacation from school.

Checking himself out in the mirror, Carlos was impressed with what he saw — kind of anyway. Lots of guys had whitey-tighties. Well, maybe not lots but at least some of them did. The boy needed something to make his stand out. Then again, other superheroes wore their underwear over tights; some even donned matching capes. Carlos was the only superhero who wore his drawers in an ordinary fashion. Maybe his costume would stand out after all.

If only the school, his probation officer, the cops, and his parents would get over their hypocritical judgment of him — claiming running through the halls in his costume was indecent exposure. It wasn't like he paraded around in his birthday suit!

What was wrong with being seen in his underwear? If people could dress in a similar fashion at swimming pools, in wrestling tournaments, and in bodybuilding competitions, school shouldn't be any different.

A knock came to the door. "Yeah?" the superhero called.

His door swung open before he had a chance to cover himself up. Ma and Pop both barged in.

"Can't you knock first?" Carlos asked while throwing his sweats back on.

Ma laughed sarcastically, "Oh, so it's embarrassing for your parents to catch you without your pants on but it's perfectly comfortable jogging around in front of your classmates and teachers that way?"

Carlos plopped himself down on the bed and peered out the window — no reporters in sight! He wondered how far his story might spread. Hopefully it wouldn't just stop with the local papers; his name deserved to be echoed off of every building in the nation.

"Why, Carlos?" Pop interrupted his train of thought. "I want to know why you thought that was okay?"

The teen returned his focus to the conversation at hand. "We already talked about this at the school," he replied coldly.

"Right," Pop replied. "You were questioned by the police … but your answers weren't genuine. What was whirling around that empty head of yours?"

Carlos pulled his legs up on the bed and laid down, facing away from his parents. Discussing the past wouldn't magically erase it from history.

Ma was losing her patience. Snapping her fingers, she yelled, "Sit up!... You don't look the other way when an adult is speaking to you!"

At the pace of a slug traipsing through peanut butter, the careless teen raised up and made eye contact with his mother. "You guys are acting like it's the end of the world... It's not like I glued sandpaper to Aunt Maggie's toilet seat again!"

It took everything in Pop to keep his voice calm, "Carlos," he said, "you've crossed the line, my boy. If the court system doesn't take drastic measures, your ma and I will."

"Meaning?"

"We're not sure yet. We're still weighing all of our options."

"Like what?"

Ma teared up, "Probably something along the lines of a military academy or a boarding school."

If nothing else had gotten his attention, that sure did! Carlos put his feet back on the floor and stood up. "You don't want me anymore?"

Ma left the room, too choked up to speak.

Pop motioned for the boy to return to his seat. "We love you, son. But we're extremely concerned. If you don't start taking things seriously, you're going to hurt somebody."

Carlos snickered, "I'm not violent, Pop. You know that."

Pop sat down next to the teen. "I'm not referring to that type of hurt. I'm talking about violating someone. We don't want you abusing one of your classmates or worse, someone younger than you are."

Twiddling his thumbs, Carlos spoke in a soft voice, "I can't believe you think I'd do something like that."

"I don't want to believe it," Pop replied. "But you keep taking things further and further. It started with clipping half-naked women out of magazine ads, then you graduated to pornographic websites, you asked that girl at school if she was a virgin, you told people you heard your ma and I—"

"Okay, Pop!" Carlos exclaimed. "I don't need any more examples. I get it."

"I hope you do, son. Your ma and I are determined to put a stop to this before things get worse."

The boy felt as if his world was quickly coming to an end. "So, you want to ship me off somewhere? To pretend I'm not a part of the family?"

"Carlos, you will always be a member of our family. But you need more help than we know how to give." The man's eyes screamed of heartbreak and shame.

"Can't you just give me another chance?" Carlos asked.

"You've had too many chances already, son."

"Sounds to me like you've already made up your mind."

Pop sat quietly for a moment looking as though he didn't know what to say. The situation was more than awkward for him. "You're right, Carlos," he said. "We have. Your ma and I are not comfortable allowing you to continue staying here. You won't be welcome under this roof until you've gotten your hormones under control. The court system may decide to place you in a long-term psychiatric hospital or a detention center for sexual offenders. If they do, we're not going to fight it... If they don't, however, we're going to find another placement for you."

Carlos hugged his old man — not because he appreciated what was being said. He knew hugs had a way of warming a parent's heart. "I'm sorry," he said. "I won't do it again."

"It's too late for that now, son. What's done is done."

Releasing his tight grip on Pop, Carlos looked him in the eye, "Can I at least have some say-so as to where I go?"

"You can make suggestions, but the final decision will be up to your ma and I."

"I understand," the boy replied. "But can I go somewhere out in the country? Like one of those boys' ranches where I can ride horses and milk cows? I've always wondered what it would be like to live on a farm."

Pop shook his head, "You don't get it, do you son? We're not trying to reward you for acting out! You've got to learn some boundaries!"

2

Inviting a detective who was accompanying a social worker from Child Protective Services into his living room was difficult, but Mr. Estrada felt he had no choice. Even though they didn't have a warrant, the social worker insisted she had the right to enter their home for the purposes of conducting a full investigation.

Mr. Estrada didn't understand. He thought government employees had no rights to enter private dwellings without first obtaining a court order to do so — the detective insisted that was not the case.

"Let me explain the reason for our visit," the social worker said after obtaining permission to step inside. "Your son's behavior is of the utmost concern. When we receive referrals like this one, we have to ensure the offending juvenile has a safe home environment."

"I understand," Mr. Estrada replied.

"I would like to begin my assessment by speaking with Carlos," the lady said. "Is there a room where I can interview him alone?"

Carlos squirmed nervously.

He wasn't the only one who was uncomfortable. Mr. Estrada wanted to tell the officials to hit the road and that he didn't care if the door hit them where the good Lord split them. It was his home, his castle and his domain. As a citizen of the United States of America he felt he had the right to decide what took place there. But they had already been through all of that. The freedom he thought he had was all but a myth.

Still, if he could prevent Carlos from having to be alone with her, it would at least relieve some of the tension in the room. "Our son doesn't like to be questioned by adults he doesn't know," he said. "Even when we go to doctors or to see his probation officer, he wants me or his Ma to be present with him."

The social worker casually pushed a strand of hair out of her face. "We can't take any chances. If you or his mother are in the room, Carlos may not be comfortable disclosing the truth about any abuse or neglect that may be occurring here."

The picture was becoming more clear. "So, you're here to see if my wife and I are abusive?"

The social worker nodded, "Afraid so."

"Unreal! Unbelievable! Our son gets in trouble, so you come out here to interrogate his parents?"

"I'm just doing my job, sir. Do you have a place where I can interview him alone or would you prefer I take him down to my office?"

That lady meant business. Mr. Estrada could tell standing up to her was only going to spell more trouble than it was worth. "You can do it here," he grumbled. "Carlos, why don't you take this lady to your room?"

The thirteen-year-old stood with his legs trembling beneath him. "I'm sorry, guys," he said with his eyes moving back and forth between Ma and Pop.

"You didn't do anything wrong," the social worker assured him.

"He didn't?" Mr. Estrada scoffed. "Why are you here, then?"

Ignoring him, the social worker said, "Show me to your room, Carlos."

Once the coast was clear, the detective spoke up, "While Sonya's with your son, I will need to speak with each of you individually. Who wants to go first?"

Mr. and Mrs. Estrada looked at each other, neither looking forward to an interrogation.

"I suppose I'll go first," Mrs. Estrada said.

"We can do the interview right here if your husband is willing to leave the room."

Mr. Estrada did not like the situation one bit. He didn't know the detective from Cain. Just because the man wore a badge didn't mean he was a good guy. For all he knew, the so-called detective could be a sexual predator or a serial killer.

When Mr. Estrada didn't budge, the detective became slightly more aggressive. "Would you mind leaving the room?"

Mr. Estrada did mind — more than that brazen detective would ever know. Determined to control his emotions, he simply said, "No problem... I'll be in the garage if you need me."

With his stomach in knots, Mr. Estrada stepped outside. For years, he had heard horror stories about Child Protective Services. The word on the street was that social workers were awarded bonus checks for removing a certain number of children from their homes each month. If that were the case, a dishonest social worker would have good reason to twist anything he, his wife, or son said.

According to Mr. Estrada's cell phone, it was 9:00 am. He wondered how long his family was going to be subjected to questioning.

Noticing how sloppy his garage had gotten, he thought about trying to tidy it up a bit, but that sick feeling taking over his body made it impossible to do anything but hop in the car to impatiently await his interview.

At 10:30 am, the detective finally made his way to the garage. "Thank you for your patience," he said.

"No problem," Mr. Estrada replied, getting out of his vehicle. "Do you want me to come back inside with you?"

"No, that's okay. We can talk here. Just so you will be aware, I will be taping this conversation."

This situation was more serious than Mr. Estrada thought. The only reason for taping the interview was because the officer planned on using it at a later time — Mr. Estrada wasn't stupid. Afraid to object, he quietly said, "Understood."

The detective took a small notepad out of his shirt pocket and flipped to a fresh page. "I'd like to begin by having you describe your son's personality for me. What's Carlos like?"

Mr. Estrada faked a smile, "He's a sweet, fun kid. Almost always has a grin on his face. I'd say he's somewhat of a people-pleaser… when he's not being ornery anyway."

"And your wife. What's she like?"

At least the guy's questions weren't laced with arsenic. It almost felt as though he was simply trying to find out how each member of the family viewed the others in their household. That was easy enough! "She's the best thing that ever happened to me," Mr. Estrada said. "Supportive and loving, a hard worker, amazing sense of humor."

The detective was apprehensive. "I see. So, you have a perfect family? Everybody gets along well? Never a squabble or fight?"

Mr. Estrada could tell he had said the wrong thing. "I'm not claiming there are never problems, sir. My wife and I have disagreements from time to time. And Carlos... he's a teenager. The boy wouldn't be normal if he didn't get in his fair share of trouble."

The detective jotted something down on his notepad. "Trouble, huh? And who deals with him when he gets in trouble? In other words, who is the primary disciplinarian? You or your wife?"

Mr. Estrada thought for a moment, sticking to his game-plan of producing no hasty answers. "I don't know that either of us is the primary disciplinarian. It's pretty even."

"Uh-huh," the detective said. "And what kind of consequences do you give your son?"

Mr. Estrada's breathing shallowed but there wasn't a thing he could do about it. "I... uh... I've grounded him, assigned extra chores, sent him to bed early, taken away privileges... you know, the same types of discipline all parents give their kids."

"And would that *same type of discipline* include corporal punishment?"

Mr. Estrada leaned against the car, "Yes, sir. It would."

A sneaky expression lit the detective's face. "Would you mind defining corporal punishment? What does it mean to you?"

Mr. Estrada shrugged his shoulders, "It doesn't mean the same thing to everybody?"

"No, sir. It sure doesn't."

What did the way he disciplined Carlos have to do with the boy running around the school in his underwear? Did the detective seriously believe he had abused his son and that's why he was acting out? What an infuriating interview! Mr. Estrada didn't want to, but he knew he had to answer. "I believe it refers to spankings, sir."

"So, you readily admit to hitting your son?"

Oh, the nerve! That was exactly what Mr. Estrada was afraid of. Some liberal minded cop who probably didn't have any kids of his own who had no idea how effective the rod of correction could be. Somehow, he had to keep himself calm. He could not insult the man, regardless of how he felt. "Not hitting. Spanking, sir."

"Spanking, hitting, same difference," the detective mumbled. "Using your terminology then, will you admit to spanking your son?"

"Yes, sir. Spankings are still legal, are they not?"

"They are as long as they're not abusive."

"And where is the line drawn? How do you decide what kind of a spanking is discipline and what kind is abusive?"

Apparently, the detective hadn't taken any courses in multi-tasking. He took his time in scribbling down another note and didn't speak a word until he was finished. Finally, he looked up. "As long as you haven't been excessive, you have nothing to worry about."

Mr. Estrada decided to learn from the detective. If the man could make him define corporal punishment, he could make him define some terms as well. "And what is the definition of excessive?" he asked.

The detective stammered for a moment, "I... uh... well, the law isn't clear on that. It's a judgment call."

Somehow, Mr. Estrada wasn't surprised. Sounded like a dump truck load of horse manure as far as he was concerned.

"So, if you like me, you can say it's discipline, and if you don't, you can claim it's excessive?"

"Sir, we don't have all day. Let's just continue on with the interview… Does your wife spank Carlos as well?"

Mr. Estrada thought about insisting on an answer to his question before allowing the interview to continue but he knew it would only make matters worse. "Yes, she does."

"Now these spankings, are they limited to his backside or is contact made with any other part of his body?"

Mr. Estrada chuckled sarcastically. "What kind of interview is this? Are you accusing me of beating my son?"

The detective spoke in a voice rattled with annoyance, "I'm not accusing you of anything, sir; I'm simply collecting information."

Collecting information for what reason? To separate the members of a family? To press assault charges? Argh! Mr. Estrada couldn't wait for his uninvited guests to go back to wherever it was they had come from. He answered his question with a dry tone, "We only spank his behind, sir."

The detective turned up the heat, making it even more apparent that he was on a mission, "Do both of you spank with your bare hands or with an object of some kind?"

Mr. Estrada looked the detective over. His name tag said "Detective Olson." Sure enough, the man had handcuffs. He saw where this was headed.

"Are you going to answer the question?" Detective Olson asked.

"Sorry," Mr. Estrada replied. "We used to spank him with our hands but as he's gotten older and that's become less effective, we've begun using other things."

"Specifics please," the detective prodded.

It wasn't that Mr. Estrada had done anything wrong, but it was clear he and Detective Olson were not on the same page. Stumbling through his words, he said, "My wife prefers using... a wooden spoon... I generally apply the belt."

Detective Olson examined Mr. Estrada's wide leather belt with a careful eye. "A moment ago, you claimed the only part of your son's body to affected by corporal punishment is his backside. Do you mean to tell me the belt never wraps around? It never connects with anything but his bottom?"

Beads of sweat popped up on Mr. Estrada's forehead. "Should I have an attorney present for these questions?"

"No, sir. There's no need in that." The detective looked toward the garage door for a moment. "You're not under arrest or anything... Look, I can see you're getting upset. Why don't we just speed this thing up a bit? Is Carlos always fully clothed when he gets spanked?"

Mr. Estrada's chest began to pound. More sweat droplets made their way to his forehead. His legs felt as though they were about to give out from under him. Still, he had to answer, and honestly, "Most of the time... well, sometimes anyway... but not always."

Detective Olson looked at him as if he were a criminal, "You understand your son is thirteen, right?"

"Yes, sir. I'm perfectly aware of my son's age." Mr. Estrada replied.

"And you understand that boys in their early teens go through puberty and their hormones are raging?"

Did the man think he was a complete idiot? It's not like Mr. Estrada had never been a teenager himself! Detective Olson was beginning to get to him if he hadn't already. "Yes, sir. I get that," he said.

"Yet you see nothing wrong with forcing him to expose himself so you or your wife can spank him?"

Mr. Estrada chuckled nervously, "To be honest, no; I don't see anything wrong with making him drop his pants so he can feel the full effect of the discipline we are implementing."

"Other than when he's spanked, are there ever other occasions when you or your wife see him less than fully clothed?"

"No, sir," Mr. Estrada said.

"So, you always knock before entering his room?"

The Estrada family's interrogation went on for hours. When all was done and over with, the social worker thanked them for putting up with all of their questions.

"So, what happens next?" Mrs. Estrada asked.

"Detective Olson and I will compare notes with one another. We may also speak with neighbors and other individuals who might have any information to share with us. We should have our investigation completed within a couple of weeks."

3

Of the many duties his position entailed, the one Philip Bones despised more than any other was attending court hearings.

Seated next to him was Sonya Rowlands from Child Protective Services. Most of the time when Philip saw her in a courtroom, it meant bad news was about to peek its head above the horizon. On the other side of Ms. Rowlands was an officer Philip didn't recognize.

The probation officer watched nervously as Thomas Lowry, a public defender, escorted his client in from the back of the room. Not too far behind them, the teenager's parents dragged themselves through the door with bags under their eyes and wadded up tissues in hand.

As everyone took their seats, the door to the judge's chamber opened. "Will all please rise for the seating of the Honorable Judge Kevin Williams?" the bailiff asked.

Everyone in the room grew silent as they stood to their feet. "Thank you," the bailiff said. "You may be seated."

The judge announced they were meeting to hear the case of the state versus Carlos Estrada.

Philip cringed. He didn't have a good feeling about the hearing, and it hadn't even taken off yet.

"Carlos, this is an informal hearing, so you can stay in your seat," Judge Williams said. "Son, please explain to the court what you did to get yourself suspended from school."

Carlos grinned, "It was kind of a dumb thing to do, but I came up with my own superhero costume and ran in and out of classrooms showing it off."

"And can you describe this costume to the court?"

An uneasy smile spread across the probation officer's face. He would hate to be in that boy's shoes!

Surprisingly, Carlos didn't seem the least bit nervous, "I can show everybody if you want me to."

Judge Williams put his hand up, "No, that would not be appropriate. Please describe the costume to the court."

"Yes, sir..." Carlos replied. "It was my underwear."

Judge Williams didn't crack the faintest smile. He simply said, "Thank you, Carlos... Now, did you carry your costume from room to room or how exactly did you show it off?"

"I didn't take them off!" Carlos laughed as if that were the most ridiculous question he had ever heard. "I just slid my pants off and ran around in my underwear."

Philip watched the judge's face. The man must have eaten steel for breakfast. His face showed no emotion as he continued his questioning, "Did one of your classmates put you up to this or did you come up with the idea on your own?"

"They wished they thought of it!" Carlos snickered. "Even if they had, they'd have never had the guts to act on it."

"I see… And Carlos, you're already on probation for a prior conviction of sending inappropriate photos to females. Is that correct?"

"Yes, sir."

The judge turned his attention to the social worker from Child Protective Services. "Ms. Rowlands, I understand you've had the opportunity to visit the home of this client. Is that correct?"

Ms. Rowlands leaned forward, "Yes, Your Honor, I have."

"Based on that visit, what are your recommendations in regards to this case?"

Sonya took her job a little too seriously as far as Philip was concerned. The woman thrived on wrapping judges around her little finger. In pretty much every hearing Philip had ever attended, whatever that little lady said is what went. "Your Honor," she replied, "I do not feel this client is improving his behaviors while on probation; I believe he needs to spend time in a juvenile detention center. Furthermore, Carlos should not be permitted to return to his parents' custody until they have completed a minimum of three months of parental counseling."

Judge Williams looked at the paperwork in front of him. "And why is that, Ms. Rowlands?"

"Your Honor, Mr. and Mrs. Estrada haven't the foggiest idea of how to properly parent a child like Carlos. Even after years of deviant conduct, they did not request a psychiatric evaluation to be performed on him until his probation officer ordered it. They do not currently take him to counseling. Carlos says his parents beat him on a regular basis. Your Honor, the state does not feel it's in the boy's best interests for him to reside with his parents at this time."

Philip concentrated on looking at the judge. He did not want to make eye contact with the woman sitting next to him

17

for fear she would somehow read his thoughts; they weren't very pretty.

The judge turned to the officer sitting on the other side of Ms. Rowlands, "Detective Olson, you interviewed Mr. and Mrs. Estrada, and it's my understanding that you also spoke with Carlos. Are your findings in agreement with those of Ms. Rowlands?"

From the expression on Detective Olson's face, Philip assumed the man felt the same way about Ms. Rowlands that he did. "Partially, Your Honor," the detective began. "I am in full agreement that the minor needs to be incarcerated in order to fully understand the gravity of his actions. Where I disagree with Ms. Rowlands, however, is in regards to the child's parents. When interviewing them, I immediately found myself taken back by their old-fashioned views of child-rearing. As Ms. Rowlands mentioned, Carlos is not in counseling. However, the Estradas have tried that approach in the past and found it ineffective.

"Ms. Rowlands referenced Carlos being beaten on a regular basis. No one I interviewed ever used the word *beat*. This family utilizes various forms of discipline; one of the methods they choose to employ is corporal punishment. I can't say I personally would ever spank a teenager, but part of what makes America a great nation is our right to freedom. Parents have the right to discipline their children in accordance with their beliefs. Carlos did not leave me with the impression he fears his parents or that he feels they're abusing him. The Estradas appear to be doing everything they can for their son. I see no grounds for removing him from their custody. From a legal standpoint, Carlos should be placed in a correctional facility for his criminal act of indecent exposure. Once he serves his time, I believe he should be free to return to the care of Mr. and Mrs. Estrada."

Philip wanted to smirk but fought to keep his emotions hidden deep inside of him. It was a good thing because the judge was staring him right in the eyeball. "Now I'd like to hear from our juvenile probation officer... Mr. Bones, you've been overseeing this young man's probation. What is your take on everything the court has heard?"

Philip made eye contact with Carlos and his parents. This was the part of the hearing he detested the most. "Your Honor, I must side with Detective Olson in this case. I believe the Estradas are doing everything in their power to control their son, but Carlos refuses to take matters seriously. I too feel he would benefit from a short term in a juvenile detention center. However, it should be noted that said facility should be equipped to handle sexual offenders."

Judge Williams glanced at his notes. "Mr. Lowry, it looks like I failed to call upon you. As the public defender for Carlos Estrada, is there any additional pertinent information the court should be made aware of or do you have any objections to anything that has been presented?"

Mr. Lowry and Carlos took turns whispering back and forth for a moment before the attorney said, "No, sir... I am in full agreement with seeing my client temporarily housed in a juvenile detention center. I truly feel it would be in his best interests."

"In that case," Judge Williams said, "the court hereby sentences Carlos Estrada to serve ninety-days in a juvenile correctional facility with the opportunity of an early release: a hearing will be scheduled approximately thirty days from today. The court finds no fault on behalf of Mr. or Mrs. Estrada and finds no just cause to order parental counseling at this time."

"But Your Honor—," Ms. Rowlands interjected.

Judge Williams brought his gavel down, "No, Ms. Rowlands. You have already had your say! My decision is final."

Philip was stunned at seeing a judge actually stand up to the ever-so-powerful Sonya Rowlands. He wouldn't mind seeing that happen a little more frequently.

4

Sitting in the back of the squad car with his hands behind his back and his feet shackled had to have been the most horrifying moment of Carlos Estrada's life. Juvie was supposed to be for teens who got caught shoplifting, who tried to kill people, stole cars and took them for joyrides... not for him. Not for a kid whose worst crime was taking his pants off and running through the halls of his school. It wasn't fair!

Carlos refused to look out the window. He didn't want to see smiling faces. He had no desire to watch other kids laughing and joking in the backseats of their family automobiles. He didn't want to see the beautiful weather he would no longer have the opportunity to enjoy. He would rather keep his eyes closed and continue tuning out the officer who continuously asked him if he was okay.

What a stupid question to keep asking! Didn't the tears flowing down his cheeks answer it anyway? Of course, he wasn't okay! He had just been stolen away from his family and was about to be locked up with some juvenile delinquents he had no desire to be around. Why was this happening? It was a nightmare he couldn't wake up from!

The cruiser pulled into a tiny garage. The thirteen-year-old thought his heart was going to stop. He looked through the back glass just in time to see the garage door closing behind them.

Two police officers entered the garage through doors that led into an ugly brick building. His driver got out and unlocked the back door. "Get out," he said.

Carlos assumed he was at the juvenile detention center. He wanted to ask but at the same time had no desire to speak. As a matter of fact, he was too afraid to get out. Couldn't he just sleep in the back of the car? At least he knew he was safe.

The driver grabbed his arm and firmly pulled him out of the vehicle. "Don't give us any trouble now," he said.

Carlos still didn't speak. He allowed the three officers to lead him inside the building. It was obvious the staff had been expecting him. A lady came around a counter to start the intake process. The driver took the shackles and handcuffs off of him while the lady took his name, date of birth, address, and telephone number. She would have taken his social security number as well, but he had still not taken the time to memorize it. The lady fingerprinted him and then motioned for a male officer.

He was one rough-looking dude. Carlos worried that perhaps he was an escaped inmate who had killed an officer and was pretending to be someone he wasn't. Those tattoos on his neck were hideous. And his shiny bald head — what was up with that? He tried not to stare, but the guy had a fat mole growing out of his eyebrow.

"This way," he ordered. Carlos accompanied the man down another hallway where a second male officer joined them.

"Strip," the first one said.

Somehow taking his clothes off in front of two police officers who were ordering him to do so didn't quite give him the same rush as sporting his superhero costume at school. Carlos was so scared he began to cry. The officers didn't mind. They looked at each other and smiled.

"Not so tough now, is he?" one of them said.

"Bet you wish you would have obeyed the law, huh, kid?" the other one asked. "Hope this is a lesson to you. You don't ever want to come back to this place."

He could say that again! Carlos had his shoes and socks off. He wasn't in a hurry to go any further than that. He just wished someone would pinch him so he could escape the ferocious nightmare.

"Hurry up, kid!" one of the officers demanded.

That was easy for him to say! He wasn't a little boy being harassed by two strange men. Carlos slipped his shirt off over his head and tossed it on the floor. Another tear trickled down his cheek. He just wanted the whole thing to be done and over with. He could do this. He really could. It would be over in no time. Whatever was going to happen just was. He had to do it.

Slowly, he unfastened his jeans and pulled them off. He stood back up and made eye contact with one of the officers.

"The faster you move, the faster you can get into your cell!"

That wasn't exactly what Carlos had been hoping to hear. He was hoping more for something like, "Okay, that's far enough." But no, it wasn't that easy. He had to lose all of his clothes.

Carlos took his underwear off.

"Raise your arms straight above your head and hold them there."

Carlos felt as though he were on display — like an animal of some kind.

"Good. Now slowly turn in a complete circle."

Humiliated — that was the best word to describe how the teenager felt at that moment.

"Spread your legs shoulder width apart."

Carlos's legs began to tremble as he sheepishly complied with their commands.

"Bend over. Your fingertips need to touch the floor."

Was this really necessary? It wasn't like he was trying to smuggle a shank into the place. Who did they think he was? That's okay. It was almost over. There wasn't much more they could do to him.

"Good. Stand up. Open your mouth nice and wide for me." One of the officers used a gloved hand to move his tongue around.

After a few more minutes of annoying inspections, the officer said, "Almost finished. Shower time."

Carlos shook his head. "I don't need one."

"That's our decision. Walk over there and stand behind the black line."

Any dignity Carlos had was long gone. He followed the officer's instructions and tried to stand tall as the officers blasted him with a powerful hose. The water wasn't ice-cold, but it was anything but warm.

Once the hose cut off, an officer threw him a towel. Before he got himself fully dried off, the officer tossed him some clothes, "Get dressed."

"I can wear my own clothes," Carlos protested.

"Again, that's for us to decide. Put them on."

Carlos glared at the man through eyes of brokenness. He held up the boxer shorts. "These are too big."

The officer couldn't have cared less. "Get dressed, now!"

Carlos put the oversized underwear on and then the repulsive gray and navy-blue jumpsuit.

5

The first sermon Philip preached at Freedom Baptist Church went wonderfully. Somehow, he felt more comfortable there than he had at his home church. Perhaps it was just the fact that the young preacher boy had gotten a tiny bit of experience under his belt. Whatever it was, he wasn't complaining.

On his way out of church that night, Brother Michaels, the deacon who had asked him to preach their evening services, invited him and Billy to join his family for dinner at the Riverbend Café, a new little restaurant that had recently opened up in town. Knowing Billy wouldn't complain about free food, Philip gladly accepted the invitation.

On the way to the café, the probation officer quizzed his protégé on the sermon and was surprised to find out how much the teen had retained. "I am impressed," Mr. Bones told him. "Not only did you keep your commitment to coming to church with me this evening, but you paid attention."

Billy grinned, "You preached a lot better than you did the first time, Mr. Bones," he said. "If you keep getting behind the pulpit, you might actually get good at it."

Mr. Bones laughed, appreciating the bond he and his fourteen-year-old client were finally beginning to form.

Once they got to the café, the probation officer sat between Billy and Brother Michaels. Across the table from him was an interesting looking young lady he had not yet had the privilege of meeting — she appeared to be close to his age but her flower-print dress belonged to someone much older.

Philip reached his hand across the table, "I'm Mr. Bones... uh, I mean, Philip."

Lisa's face colored as she took his hand in hers. To his surprise, instead of shaking it, she gently turned it over and examined his palm. "I'm Ms. Michaels... uh, I mean, Lisa," she giggled.

Philip didn't know what to think of that but Billy sure did. It took him so much off guard that he started to laugh, preventing him from swallowing his soda. Covering his mouth, he hoped he wouldn't erupt like a volcano. Everyone at the table was cracking up as his face reddened. Alden couldn't hold it in — his lips popped open and soda hit his hand before making its way onto the table in front of him. How humiliating!

Darlene, their waitress, stopped by just as he wiped his mouth on his sleeve. "Are we ready to order?"

Brother Michaels looked around the table, "I believe so. Ladies, why don't you go first?"

Mrs. Michaels stalled for a moment as she struggled to choose between lasagna and chicken fried steak — the steak won her heart. Lisa, on the other hand... she was different alright. "Is it okay if I order off of the children's menu?" she asked.

Darlene smiled, "Sure. What would you like?"

"Do I have to order it exactly as it's printed or can I make it my own?"

Philip had no idea what the young lady could possibly need to customize from the kids' menu, but he was about to find out.

"Tell us what you want, and we'll do the best we can," Darlene told her.

"Thank you. You're so sweet!... So, I always like to try new things and I was looking at the mac and cheese... which sounds absolutely di-vine. But that peanut butter and jelly sandwich is screaming my name and saying 'pick me, pick me!' and oh, it's such a difficult decision. I—"

"Would like to order both?" the waitress asked.

"Kind of," Lisa giggled. "Could you prepare a plate of mac and cheese and drizzle some melted peanut butter across the top of it?"

Darlene raised an eyebrow, "Are you serious? Macaroni and cheese and peanut butter? Honey, are you pregnant?"

Lisa looked at her parents and then at Philip. What a thing to ask! "No, I'm not pregnant," she said, "just a girl with a style of her own."

"You can say that again," Brother Michaels agreed. "That daughter of mine. Sometimes I think Lisa must have been switched at birth. She definitely doesn't take after her mother or me."

Darlene turned to face the kitchen for a second, appearing to be either deep in thought or possibly trying to hide her true feelings about her customer's weirdness. After a few seconds, she said, "Okay... so macaroni and cheese covered with melted peanut butter? I'll see what the cooks can do."

Philip glanced around the table. Mr. and Mrs. Michaels were both smiling from ear to ear. Philip assumed they were embarrassed, although it was possible they were amused. Billy, on the other hand, had a mischievous look on his face. "I'll have what she's having," he piped up.

Philip couldn't believe his ears. It was humiliating enough to have one person at the table place such a ridiculous order, but two? Philip shook his head. It was going to be an interesting evening.

While they were waiting on their food to arrive, Lisa asked Philip what he did outside of normal working hours. "Like, do you have any hobbies or anything?" she asked.

"I don't really have time for that," Philip replied. "I guess you could say working with young men like Billy here has become my favorite pastime. How about you?"

"I have a lot of interests," Lisa said. "But I would have to say my favorite hobby is sculpting."

"Really? That's different. What do you sculpt?"

Lisa giggled, "Oh, anything and everything. Sailboats, people, buildings. I've done a little of everything."

"Wow! I would love to see your work sometime. Do you sculpt from rock?"

"Oh, no!" Lisa replied. "I like having a wide variety of colors to work with. I don't like to work with stone because it doesn't offer much versatility. You know what I mean? Like you're kind of stuck with whatever you design the first time. That's just not for me… I prefer materials with qualities that are more modifiable. That's why I decided to become a playdough artist."

That did it! There was no way Philip could possibly maintain his composure. A playdough artist? Where did this girl come up with her ideas? Lisa was not exaggerating when she said she had her own unique style — that was for certain. Philip made it a point to minimalize further conversation with the odd duck throughout the remainder of their meal.

Shortly after they ate, Brother Michaels spoke up, "Philip, I have a proposition for you."

"What's that?"

"I told you our church is without a pastor right now. That's why I've asked you to fill in for our evening services."

"Right," Philip said.

"I believe it would help our church to have consistency in leadership during this transition period. As we discussed in your office, you're not qualified to pastor, but while we're waiting for God to send us the right man, it would be helpful if you were present for all of our services — even if you're just sitting in the pew on Sunday mornings."

Philip hadn't seen that one coming, "You're not proselytizing, are you?"

"No," Brother Michaels laughed. "Not at all. Why don't you talk to Pastor Jahmal about it and see what he thinks? If he isn't comfortable with the idea, you can just forget I ever mentioned it."

Philip agreed to give it some thought and prayer.

6

Mrs. Estrada couldn't bring herself to do anything. How was she supposed to pretend nothing was going on? That was her baby boy. Her only child. The one she had dreamed of having ever since she was a little girl.

Things weren't supposed to turn out this way. How had Carlos gone from being that adorable, sweet little boy that she used to spend hours in the park with to become some kind of sexually-driven monster?

Never in a million years had she expected to be the mother of someone who could quite possibly grow up to be a child molester or rapist. A young man who could potentially scar someone else's life forever.

She laid on her bed, wondering how her son was being treated. She knew she had the right to drop in and visit him. But she couldn't bring herself to do it. How could she see her son in a juvenile detention center? How could she ever leave there without him?

Her husband would be coming in any minute. She could only imagine how irritated he was going to be that she didn't have dinner on the table. She didn't care. Dinner was the least of her worries. Carlos could be getting beaten up while she was laying there in the comfort of her own home. Worse, a guard could be mistreating him. Maybe she should find a way to ignore her emotions and go see him.

The battle was real.

She heard the front door open. Still, she couldn't move. Something was keeping her pinned to that bed. "Honey!" Mr. Estrada called.

She wanted to answer, but nothing would come out of her mouth. Mrs. Estrada lay there waiting — for what, she didn't know. Eventually, her husband entered the room and sat on the bed next to her.

"You have to stop doing this to yourself," he said. "Carlos wouldn't want you to be upset."

Mrs. Estrada shook her head. It didn't matter what Carlos wanted. It didn't matter what her husband wanted. It didn't even matter what she wanted. All that mattered was that her son was behind bars and she could do nothing to protect him.

"We got something in the mail from Child Protective Services," Mr. Estrada told her. "Do you want to open it or should I?"

Mrs. Estrada turned her head so she could see her husband's face. "I can't," she whispered. "I don't have it in me."

Mr. Estrada opened the envelope and took out the letter. He read it out loud, "Dear Mr. and Mrs. Estrada, this letter is to bring you up to date regarding our investigation into the potential abuse and/or neglect of your son, Carlos Estrada. Unfortunately, at this time, we are not able to make a definitive ruling in this case. Temporarily, we will be placing a halt on the investigation. We're not closing the case necessarily but suspending all investigative activity for the time being. We reserve the right to reactivate the investigative process on this case any time within the next 180 days."

That letter did nothing more than add to Mrs. Estrada's emotional distress. Not only did she have to worry about Carlos, but what about her and her husband? The state could tap their phones, follow them around, pry into their personal affairs without their knowledge or consent, anytime they wanted to during the next six months. That was terrible news! Who wants to feel like they're under the government's microscope all of the time?

She began sobbing uncontrollably. Her husband laid down next to her. "Everything will be alright, honey. We're going to get through this."

After several minutes, Mrs. Estrada managed to find her voice, "What do we do when Carlos gets out?"

"Bring him home," her husband said matter-of-factly.

"And just forget everything that happened?... What if he acts out again?... We have to have a plan."

"I don't know," Mr. Estrada said. "I don't think it's even possible for us to plan ahead with this thing. Until we see how his incarceration impacts him, there's no reason to play all of the 'what-if' games.

Mrs. Estrada sat up. She wanted her son back more than anything in the world. But she wanted to make sure his best interests were served; not hers. He needed constant, close supervision. Perhaps supervision only a facility designed for juveniles like Carlos could provide. What if that social worker was right? What if she and her husband weren't prepared to handle their son? If the Estradas enabled his behaviors, they were going to continue escalating and then what?

"Do you think we should go see him? Talk to him? Try to gauge how he's doing?" she asked.

"I have been asking myself the same question. I think that would send him the wrong message," Mr. Estrada said. "Tell him that we're so attached to him that we don't know how to enforce tough-love. I know it's got to be hard being away from home. He's probably dying to see us. But that's good for him. The harder this placement is on him, the less likely he'll be to repeat the offense."

Mrs. Estrada hadn't thought of it that way. Her husband had a point.

7

Pastor Jahmal, what a guy! Philip couldn't believe how their conversation was going. "I truly believe that, Brother Philip. Faithfulness is important. But if you're going to be at Freedom Baptist Church on Sunday and Wednesday evenings, you should be there on Sunday mornings as well. You need to be all the way in or all the way out of a church. Being partially in this one and partially in that one is only going to bring contention."

Philip was confused. He had been a member of Clover Baptist for seven years. It felt as though his pastor was shoving him out of the flock. Apparently, Pastor Jahmal picked up on Philip's hesitance. "I'm not saying we don't value your membership, son. We want you to return to worship with us as soon as Freedom gets a new pastor."

Once that was settled, Philip threw his duffle bag in the car and headed to the Wamboldt place to surprise the birthday boy. Alden opened the door, "Mr. Bones! What are you doing here?"

The probation officer grinned and handed him a large gift. "I heard somebody had a birthday yesterday."

"You didn't have to get me anything!"

"Oh, but I did! Can I come in?"

Alden was tickled to death. "Sure. Grandma's in the kitchen."

Mr. Bones was thrilled to see the house still in one piece. No holes in the walls. No graffiti on the windows. No grandmother's laying on the floor holding their ribcages. The boy had come a long way.

Hearing the commotion, Mrs. Wamboldt came out. Winking at Philip, she pretended his visit was completely unexpected, "So nice of you to stop by. What do you have there, Alden?"

The fourteen-year-old knelt next to his package. "I'm about to find out," he said as he ripped the wrapping off and tore the box open. A huge grin took over his face. "A sleeping bag? Does this mean—?"

"Yes, sir! I'm taking you to the island to celebrate!"

Alden jumped up and hugged Mr. Bones, "When?"

"As soon as you get your things together, man."

"You mean, we're going tonight?"

"That's not a problem, is it? I mean, you don't have a hot date or anything, do you?"

Alden eyed his grandmother. "Grandma, is it okay if I—"

Mrs. Wamboldt giggled with delight, "Your probation officer and I have already discussed it, Alden. You're free to go. You deserve it."

Alden spun around, gave his grandma a bear hug that nearly took the wind out of her, and dashed to his room to gather his things. The boy's excitement carried over to Philip. He had enjoyed camping out with Alden before, but this time was going to be different. It was a celebration. A time when they got to hang out just for the fun of it.

"Your love for my grandson is the best gift anyone has ever given him," Mrs. Wamboldt said. "You are a very special young man."

"Thank you, ma'am. I love working with Alden. He's a great kid."

"That he is," Mrs. Wamboldt agreed. "But let's talk about you for a minute, Mr. Bones. I don't understand why you haven't found Miss Right yet. You're handsome, have a lot of money, a nice car, a strong work ethic, you're great with kids... how old are you, if you don't mind me asking?"

Philip knew where this conversation was going. Mrs. Wamboldt probably had a neighbor, friend, or relative she wanted to hook him up with. Why was everyone so determined to play matchmaker? He didn't want the conversation to take place, but he couldn't be rude to her. "I'm twenty-four," he replied.

"Twenty-four years old and never married, huh? We need to find you a wife. Anybody catch your interest lately?"

Philip laughed while shrugging his shoulders.

"Who is she?" Mrs. Wamboldt asked.

That was one thing Philip hated about himself. Somehow he always had trouble masking what was on his mind. There was no denying he had been thinking about her. But he didn't have to come right out with it either. "I don't know if I would exactly say anybody has caught my attention—"

Mrs. Wambolt smiled, "Oh, somebody has. Your face is turning red. Tell me about her."

Philip didn't even know if he liked the girl. It wasn't like she was beautiful or highly intelligent or shared the same sense of humor he had. Her father was a deacon in the church. They were both Christians. But, he hadn't been able to stop thinking about her.

"Well," he said, not wanting to speak anything negative of Lisa, "I met a sculptor the other day, and I'm still trying to figure out what I think of her."

"A female sculptor, huh? Sounds like an interesting lady."

"She is."

Alden charged into the room with a bag full of clothes, "I'm ready!"

Smiling, Philip said, "I guess we better hit the road then. I'll have him back late tomorrow evening. Unless, of course, he wants to go to church with me Sunday morning?"

Alden grinned. "Can I, Grandma? Please!"

"I don't have any problems with that."

"In that case, I'll bring him home after the Sunday morning services."

8

Alden couldn't have possibly been happier. If he could pick any dad in the world, it would definitely be none other than the man who had just bought him that sleeping bag. He would never understand what Mr. Bones saw in him, but he would forever be grateful for what the man had done for him.

"Did you bring any homework with you?" Mr. Bones asked as they got out of the boat.

Alden chuckled. "Not this time. Did you bring the work gloves?"

The two laughed. Spending a night on the island without dealing with misbehavior or work was going to be a welcome change.

"So, what are we going to do?" Alden asked.

"We're going to have ourselves a time — that's what. Have you ever been fishing?"

Alden smiled. "A long time ago. Probably when I was like four or something. I don't remember."

"Well, you're about to. Do you remember the shed where the tools were?"

Alden nodded.

"I've got a couple of poles in there. And I'm sure we won't have any trouble finding ourselves some bait."

The birthday boy wasn't sure what he thought about fishing. But it didn't matter. He was thrilled to be getting some one-on-one time with one of his favorite people in the world. The person who had helped him overcome the anger that had been controlling and ruining his life.

After getting their poles out and making sure they were still in good working order, Mr. Bones told him it was time to hunt for worms.

"How do we do that?"

Mr. Bones didn't miss a beat. "Drop down on your belly and squirm around like a worm. Holler for them. You know, 'Here, wormie, wormie, wormie. Here wormie, wormie, wormie.' They'll come right to you."

Alden snickered. "Yeah, right. You do it then."

"You don't believe me?"

Alden shook his head. "Nah, man. Can't say that I do."

"What if we both do it at the same time then?"

Alden shook his head reluctantly. Even though the thoughts of his probation officer acting like a fishing worm and calling out to them was hilarious, he couldn't bring himself to do such a thing. "I don't think so, Mr. Bones. I'm not that gullible."

"No problem," Mr. Bones said. "We can do it the normal way if you'd prefer."

"And what's that?"

"Worms love to come right up to the ground's surface and hide under anything — boards, cinderblocks, rocks… any place that's cool. If we slowly uncover them, they'll stay out just long enough for us to grab hold of them."

Now that made sense. It sounded like something Alden was certain he could handle. He soon discovered, however, that finding them wasn't the problem. Those things were fast! His probation officer seemed to be able to grab them in a heartbeat. Every time he reached for one, it disappeared beneath the soil before he could get a firm grip.

It took a while, but he eventually got the hang of it.

When they got to the lake, however, Alden was proud to figure out that he was a much better fisherman than was his role model. Within two minutes of having his line in the water, he got a bite. Somehow, instinct taught him how to set the hook. Perhaps he just remembered from when he was little. Regardless, he got his line reeled in and had caught himself a carp.

"Way to go!" Mr. Bones exclaimed. "Do you want me to get him off the hook for you or do you want to try it?"

"I've got it!" Alden said.

"Good for you, bud. Do you want to fry him over a fire or set him free?"

That was a no-brainer. "Set him free," Alden said. "That way we can catch him again some other time."

He was thankful his probation officer had left it up to him. He would have felt guilty had he actually had to kill and eat the poor thing.

Mr. Bones kept his line in the water for an hour without a single bite. During that same time period, Alden caught two more fish.

"Alright, birthday boy... I chose fishing. Now it's your turn. What do you want to do next?"

Alden would have to give that one some thought. They could swim, but they had been there and done that. The same would be true of starting a bonfire. He wanted to do something different. Create a new memory of some kind. "Can we build something?" he asked.

"We might be able to do that. What do you have in mind?"

Alden didn't have a clue. But with all of the trees on the island, he was certain he could come up with something. "How about a lean-to? Or another storage building?"

Mr. Bones chuckled, "We could try something like that, but it would probably take up every second we have here on the island. What if we try something on a bit of a smaller scale so we can get more things in?"

"Okay... like what?"

The probation officer looked around. "Have you ever tried to walk on stilts?"

"No. I can't say that I have."

"Would you like to build a set and try them out?"

Alden pictured clowns towering above the ground on their thin-legged stilts. He could see himself falling face-first and breaking his nose. "I don't know, Mr. Bones. Building them might be fun, but I doubt I could walk on them. I'd really rather not spend the weekend in the emergency room."

Mr. Bones could tell what the boy was thinking. "You won't end up in the emergency room, birthday boy. I'm not going to let that happen. We'll just raise your feet about five or six inches off of the ground. It'll be fun. You're not going to chicken out on me, are you?"

"Just five or six inches? You promise?"

"Cross my heart and hope you die."

Alden grinned. "Let's do this then!"

9

The concrete walls in his 10x10 cell were beginning to close in on him — that's the way it felt anyway. And to think, there were times when Carlos thought he had it bad at home. At least at home he got to wear his own clothes and see his family every day.

The door to his cell opened. "Off to class," a guard said.

"Class?" Carlos asked. "I go to school while I'm here?"

"That's already been explained to you. Let's go."

Carlos knew perfectly well that no one had said a word to him about school. That he would have remembered for sure! But there was no point in arguing. If he had to go, he just did. That's all there was to it.

The classroom he was taken to looked somewhat like the one he attended in public school — except for the fact that the walls were dingier, the lighting was less than adequate, there weren't any bulletin boards or decorations, two uniformed guards were in the room, and instead of being in class with students in his grade, he felt more like he was in a one-room school house with teens ranging in age from about twelve to eighteen. Other than that, that weren't many differences.

Carlos was directed to an empty desk. A cranky-looking teacher approached him. "Name?"

"Carlos Estrada."

"Hi, Carlos. I'm Mrs. Klassen and I will be your teacher throughout the time you're in lock-up. What grade are you in?"

"Eighth."

"That's what I thought. We'll bring you some materials after I take roll call."

Carlos smirked. What a stupid procedure! Taking roll call in juvie! It's not like a kid had a choice about whether or not to be present. They knew good and well that all of their students were in attendance.

"Aaron Bronx," she said a moment later.

"Present," a studious-looking kid from the back practically yelled. Carlos couldn't help but wonder what the kid was in for. He looked like a teacher's pet.

"Michael Barron," Mrs. Klassen said.

"Yo, teach!" another voice blurted out. Michael looked like he deserved to be there. He was probably the kid Carlos needed to watch out for. He wouldn't be surprised if the kid were the reason the facility did strip searches. It's hard to tell what that guy tried to sneak in. One thing was for sure; Carlos didn't want to get on his bad side.

The thirteen-year-old tried to make mental notes about who each kid was. But there was no way he was going to remember twenty-five names and keep them straight with all of those faces. They would come in time.

At the end of the roll-call one of the boys hollered, "Hey, who's the border-hopper?"

Carlos hated that term. If the kid wanted to end up on his non-friend list, he had reached his goal. Mrs. Klassen interceded before it could go any further. "Racism will not be tolerated in this classroom. If I hear any more comments like that, the offending party will be assigned two hours of homework."

That did the trick! The unruly mouth was stopped. But the looks the kid gave... it was a good thing they didn't really have the ability to kill.

Mrs. Klassen eventually made it around to Carlos's desk. "Here you go," she said. "I need you to complete pages 311 through 317 in your geography book, 295 through 305 in science, 301 through 312 in pre-algebra, and complete these worksheets for English. If you have any questions, feel free to ask — but don't expect me to hold your hand and do the work for—"

The class burst into yells and screams as a few desks were knocked over on their sides, and a small handful of kids broke out into a brawl. Mrs. Klassen stood up straight and slowly backed toward her desk as the guards rushed in to regain control of the room.

Carlos was terrified. It wasn't that he had never seen fights in public school, but this one was different. Hair was being yanked out of heads, faces were being stomped, officers were slamming people to the floor, and it was nothing less than a miracle that no one lost their life.

By the time lunch rolled around, Carlos was starving. He followed the crowd into the cafeteria which was no more attractive than the classroom he had just come out of.

The guys formed a single-file line, and the chatter began. "Hey man," a kid said. "How long you here for?"

"A few months," Carlos said. "How about you?"

"I've got a couple of weeks left. Been here for about a year."

Carlos was jealous. Not that the kid had been locked up for a year. But that he was getting ready to have his freedom restored. He refused to think about it. "So, how much longer will we be in class today?"

"We won't be."

Carlos gave him a puzzled look.

"We only go to school for four and a half hours per day."

"For real? How does that work?"

"Instead of only doing school Monday through Friday, we have Saturday school as well. Four and a half hours, six days per week."

Six days of school per week? Carlos hoped the kid was lying. Then again, it's not like he could do anything for fun on Saturdays anyway. It would be better than just sitting around his cell being bored out of his mind.

As Carlos got closer to the food window, he began to lose his appetite. He stepped to the side trying to see what that terrible smell was.

"Back in line!"

Carlos looked over his shoulder to see the balding, tattooed, creepy looking guard approaching him. "You try to cut line again, and you'll find yourself in isolation."

The guy's friendliness was astounding. It was obvious he hadn't become an officer in a juvenile detention center because he enjoyed being around kids. It probably had more to do with the fact that he enjoyed intimidating people who were smaller than him. If that were the case, he was good at his job. Carlos wasn't about to talk back to him — even though the man was clearly mistaken.

Eventually, Carlos made it to the counter where the cooks were dishing out the food. "What is this?" Carlos asked.

"Pork chops," the cook snapped.

Pork chops? Carlos was thinking it was some kind of seafood. It most certainly looked or smelled nothing like pork. She added some green beans and corn to his plate and they didn't look any more appetizing than the pork chops.

Carlos proceeded down the line toward the cups that were sitting out, assuming he was about to receive lukewarm water. To his surprise, it was extremely watered-down kool-aid.

10

By the time Sunday morning rolled around, Philip was exhausted. Between swimming, fishing, and building a pair of stilts, he and Alden had worn themselves out. Not going to bed until 2:00 am probably had something to do with his tiredness as well.

After saying good morning a few dozen times, Philip and Alden grabbed their seats. It wasn't long before a solitary finger tapped the probation officer on his shoulder. It was none other than the playdough artist herself. "Good morning, Lisa."

"Good morning. And who is this fine looking young man?"

"This is Alden... Alden, this is Lisa."

Alden glanced at her and then at Mr. Bones. "Much better," he mumbled.

"I'm sorry, what was that?" Lisa asked.

Philip shot Alden a dirty look. "Nothing important. Don't worry about it."

"Okay," Lisa said questioningly. "So, um... hey, it looks like you've been out in the sun this weekend. Nice tan."

Philip smirked, "Yeah, Alden and I spent the weekend on a little island."

"An island?... Really?... Where at?"

Alden jumped into the conversation, "Mr. Bones inherited it when his dad passed away."

Lisa's eyes widened, "You own your own island, Philip? And here I thought your life revolved around juvenile delinquents." She turned to Alden, "No offense."

"None taken," he replied.

"So, Philip," Lisa said, "I meant to tell you I really enjoyed hearing your sermon the other night. That was powerful!"

Philip couldn't decide if the deacon's daughter was flirting with him or just trying to be kind. With his client sitting right next to him, he chose to politely end the conversation by not being very talkative. "Thanks," he said. "I'm glad you enjoyed it."

"I hope I didn't creep you out with that whole macaroni and peanut butter thing over at the café."

"The café?" Alden repeated. "Are you two seeing each other?"

"No, Alden," Philip said. "Her family, Billy, and I went out to eat after the service Wednesday evening."

"So, you've met her parents?"

Philip chuckled, unsure of how to answer that question.

Lisa took care of it for him. "Actually, he met my parents before he met me. Right now, Philip and I are just in a talking stage. You know, trying to decide if we are attracted to one another."

That was news to Philip. Why was he always the last one to know things like this? He was beginning to wonder if he had again been set up. Perhaps Brother Michaels hadn't asked him to attend Sunday morning services without having an ulterior motive. He hoped Pastor Jahmal hadn't been in on it as well.

"Alden, how old are you? I'm guessing somewhere around sixteen?"

"Fourteen," Alden said with a smile.

"Wonderful! We have Sunday School classes downstairs and I teach ages fourteen and fifteen. You'll be in my class."

If Philip hadn't already been sitting on pins and needles, that really did it. Even though Alden had changed considerably, he couldn't help remember how the boy had intentionally sabotaged his relationship with Cassie. The thoughts of Alden being in class with a young lady he was potentially interested in, not that he was interested or anything, was somewhat unnerving.

"Sounds good," Alden replied. "Do we go to class now?"

"No. My dad will make the announcement when it's time. So, Alden, what do you like to do for fun?"

"Usually just hanging out at the skatepark."

Philip gave Alden a dirty look.

"I don't bully people or smoke anymore... I just go to hang out with friends."

"Don't think I won't swing by unannounced to check on you, bud," Philip said, doubting Alden was as innocent as he claimed to be. The chances of the teen hanging out at the skatepark without getting in trouble were about equal to those of a recovering alcoholic hanging out in a bar without taking a sip of beer.

"I know, I know," the fourteen-year-old said.

"Cut the kid some slack," Lisa giggled. "Do you do anything else for fun, Alden?"

"Not really."

"That's too bad. You look like the kind of guy who would have a lot of interests. Hey, have you ever tried canine glamour-shots?"

"Canine glamour-shots?" Alden repeated with a puzzled expression on his face.

He wasn't the only one. Even though Philip should have expected her to say as much, the comment took him off guard as well. He had never met anyone quite as eccentric as Lisa. What an interesting young lady she was!

"Oh, you'd love it!" Lisa exclaimed. "What kind of dog do you have?"

"What makes you think I have one?"

It was a good question, but not as far as Lisa was concerned. "Why wouldn't you? You're a teenage boy and everybody knows dogs are man's best friend."

Alden looked at her blankly.

"Wait!... You seriously don't have a dog?"

"Nah," Alden said. "My grandma's allergic."

"That's too bad. How about you, Philip? What kind of dog do you have?"

Philip shook his head, "Afraid I don't have one either."

Lisa jutted her bottom lip out. "It must be lonely being a grown man, living all by yourself, and not having a best friend... We'll have to work on that. Anyway, Alden, dogs have the most amazing personalities. Maybe I should call them dog-alities. Get it?" Lisa snickered.

Alden shot his probation officer a surprised look. "Oh, yeah, I get it," he said. "Funny."

"I'm glad you understand my humor. Believe it or not, some people don't."

"You don't say?" Alden asked in a slightly mocking voice.

"No, really, they don't." Lisa didn't seem to get the fact that Alden was making fun of her. Either that or she was so used to it, that it didn't bother her anymore. "Anyway, as I was saying, dogs love to have their pictures taken. Especially when you put them in disguise. You know... sunglasses, cowboy hats, socks, bandanas—"

Philip's curiosity was peaked. "Dogs enjoy that?" he asked.

"Oh, yes! They crave attention! You guys will have to come over to the house sometime, so I can show you some of the portraits I've done."

"Sounds like a good idea to me," Alden said.

Philip wanted to rip out the boy's tongue. He was not ready to be in a relationship yet. Even if he was, Lisa was... Lisa. She was kind of cute — not that outer beauty was all that important. She was kind and seemed easy enough to get along with. But... she wasn't the marrying type. The girl lived on her own planet. Finding polite answers in awkward social situations wasn't one of the probation officer's strong suits, but he managed. "We might be able to sometime," he said, "but not today. I've got some studying to do this afternoon."

"No problem. There's no rush or anything," Lisa replied. "Just let me know when you have time."

"I sure will," Philip said, assuring himself that time would never come. "Oh, will you look at that? The pianist is approaching the platform. Time for the service to start. You might want to find your seat." Philip was proud of himself. That was clever!

Or so he thought. "Oh!" Lisa said, "I didn't realize it was that time already. I'll just sit here behind you guys. That way, I can show Alden where our class is here in a minute."

11

Two weeks down. Two weeks until his court date. Carlos had to hang on. No matter what happened, he had to stay out of trouble. If he wanted any possibility of an early release, he could not get a single demerit. He needed a clean slate. It could happen.

The new kid across the hall was out of his head. Carlos couldn't see him, but the boy was yelling like some kind of maniac — demanding to see his attorney. It was difficult to make out what he was saying, but after so much repetition, Carlos was beginning to get the picture. The kid claimed he was locked up on bogus charges and was being mistreated by the staff. He insisted he was going to file a lawsuit against the guards and that he was going to end up owning that place.

It seemed someone was always upset. Carlos understood how they felt. He didn't like being there any more than the next guy but getting themselves all worked up over it was accomplishing absolutely nothing — unless giving all of the other inmates headaches counted for anything.

"Shut up already!" a guy from another cell shouted.

The kid was too busy having a meltdown to even hear the other guy yelling at him. A third inmate jumped into the shouting match. Carlos covered both ears. Where were the guards? Couldn't they at least supply him with a pair of earplugs? It's not like they could be used to injure anybody.

There they were. Three officers came speed-walking through the corridor. Within a matter of seconds, they barged into the boy's cell. For a few seconds, he screamed bloody-murder, insisting they were abusing him and calling out for help. It wasn't long, however, before his cell grew silent. The guards didn't come back out of his cell for a good fifteen minutes. Carlos couldn't tell what went on in there, but whatever it was, he was most appreciative.

Carlos laid on his anything-but-comfortable bed and stared at the camera mounted in the corner of his cell. He hated that thing! Somebody was undoubtedly watching his every move. If he cried, they watched his tears. If he scratched his leg, they knew about his itch. If he picked his nose, they saw his boogers.

Enough thinking about that. There had to be something more interesting to look at. The young jailbird lowered his gaze until his eyes fell on that cold, stainless steel toilet sitting in the floor. Talk about an invasion of privacy! No walls around it. No curtain. No, the other inmates couldn't see him, but any guard walking down the hall could peer right through that massive window on his door at any time.

Carlos closed his eyes. He would rather see nothing at all than to keep looking at his depressing surroundings. If only there was a way to leap back in time. A way to escape the pure torture he was being forced to endure. Prison-life was too much to bear. He didn't know if he could make it another two weeks.

That stupid superhero costume wasn't worth all of this. Never, ever again. No way, no how. He would not even think of drawing attention to himself again. No more inappropriate texts. No more pornography. No more spying on his neighbors. If he could only get out of that place, he would prove it. He would be a completely different kid!

The boy's mind began to wander back to his parents' place. He wondered how they were coping without him. Were they mourning the fact that he was in juvie or were they celebrating some alone-time without him? Some of his peers had already had multiple visits from their moms and dads in the short time he had been locked up, but his parents? Not one time had they stopped in to see how he was doing. Other kids talked about the letters their parents had sent them. Carlos? Nope. Nothing to brag about. The facility made him write a letter every day, but Ma nor Pop ever took the time to respond. There was the answer he was looking for. His folks weren't mourning his absence. They were glad he was gone.

A tear formed in the corner of his eye. Carlos rolled over and faced the wall opposite the door, hoping no one traveling the corridor would be able to see him crying. He hated crying. He had done enough of that in the two weeks. By now those tear ducts should have been raw.

How on earth did Mr. Bones, that annoying social worker, her detective friend, and the judge expect this to help him? What did they want to do? Throw him into a bout of mental depression? The system was set up for real criminals — not for kids like Carlos.

His door flung open, "Rec time."

Carlos didn't budge. He had no desire to go to rec time. This was one time he was completely content being alone. He didn't want any physical activity. He had no desire to talk to any of the other guys. He just wanted to be left alone.

"Let's go, Estrada," the officer's voice thundered.

Carlos sat up and looked at him with tears flowing down his face. "Quit that boo-hooing and get on your feet."

The emotionally charged teen had some things he felt like saying to that officer, but he couldn't — not if he wanted any chance whatsoever of getting an early release. Choosing to play it safe, he didn't open his mouth at all but simply got out of bed and followed the officer into and down the corridor.

Thirty-minutes of fresh air. Carlos could handle it. At least he knew they wouldn't actually make him do anything. If he wanted to just sit on the sidewalk and pout, he could. As a matter of fact, he planned on doing just that.

As soon as he made it out of the building, he found himself a nice little self-pity corner. Plopping down, he rested his head on his hands. The past two weeks had went by slower than all get out. The next two would probably be even worse. He would undoubtedly witness more fights, more temper tantrums, more new kids coming in with chips on their shoulders, and more heartache every time one of his peers received visitors.

The maniac who had been screaming in his room sat down next to him. "They still haven't got my attorney for me," he said. "They're going to pay."

Carlos didn't feel up to talking. He wanted the boy to go away. He had enough negativity of his own to deal with.

"Hello? Are you deaf?"

"Sorry," Carlos said. "I've got a lot on my mind."

"Who doesn't?... Maybe you should get an attorney too. We can do a class-action suit. The more people we get involved, the more dough we can rake in."

Carlos looked at the kid as if he was a complete moron.

"I take it you're not interested?"

Carlos shook his head.

"You know why they put me in here?"

What was with this kid? Carlos only had thirty minutes of sunshine. How could he think about his own problems if the boy wouldn't close his trap? Violence rarely seemed like a valid option, but at the moment, the thought of knocking a few teeth out seemed a very realistic possibility.

No, he couldn't. That early release possibility was only two weeks away. It was no time to blow it. Not now. "Why's that?" he asked in the most disinterested voice he could possibly muster.

"For stabbing my brother."

"Nice," Carlos said.

"He had it coming. Thought just because Mom left him in charge that he could hog the remote. That ain't cool with me. You know what I'm saying?"

The kid sounded stupider all the time. He was difficult to tolerate, but somehow Carlos had to manage. "Yeah, I get you," he said.

"My brother, man, you should've seen him! He didn't see it coming at all. I came over and sat next to him on the couch. Asked him one last time if he could let me watch something. He said no, and I just pulled out that knife and jabbed it right into his belly button."

Carlos looked up at the cloud that was quickly making its way to block the sun. "I'm sure he never expected that one. That's for sure."

"You should have saw the blood, man. It got all over the couch. His eyes got as wide as golf balls. Mom came back in just as he hit the floor. Lucky for him, she called 9-1-1 and they were able to keep him alive. I don't know how long he'll live though. Mom either for that matter. Thinkin' it's okay to be snitches. I'll get out of here and I'll show them. You just wait and see."

Somehow Carlos didn't believe a single word the kid was saying. He thought it more probable that he had ended up in juvie for skipping school or being a chronic runaway. Sure didn't seem to be the killing type. Probably all mouth and no bite.

12

Time sure has a way of flying by — especially when you're having fun. A whole month had passed since Carlos Estrada was sent away to a juvenile detention center. Receiving an excellent report from the facility, Judge Williams granted him parole.

It was time for the boy's first check-in; Mr. Bones could only hope it would go well.

"Good afternoon," the probation officer said as Carlos and Mr. Estrada took their seats.

"Afternoon," Carlos replied. His father nodded without uttering a word.

"How are things going, bud?"

"I've been doing good," the ex-con said before turning his eyes toward his father, "but Ma and Pop are still trying to get rid of me."

Pop's eyes sank to the floor.

Mr. Bones attempted to hide his disappointment. "I'm not sure what you're talking about. Mr. Estrada, would you mind explaining?"

Mr. Estrada pushed his fingers through his hair and looked up. "Yes, sir. Before the court hearing, we made it clear that Carlos would not be welcome under our roof until he truly gets why it's wrong to do things that are... you know... disturbing."

Picking up an ink pen, Philip began rolling it between his palms. He slowly shifted his eyes between the father and son sitting across from him as he attempted to gauge their emotions. "Are you considering having him move in with a relative or what's the plan?"

"We don't have a plan, yet. We're still trying to figure things out."

"You do realize Carlos cannot cross state lines without my consent?"

"Yes, sir. We understand."

Mr. Bones leaned back in his chair. "Would you mind telling me what options you're considering?"

Mr. Estrada took a deep breath. "We're at a loss, Mr. Bones. The biggest issue is his schooling. We don't want Carlos in class with other students. We don't know what he might say or do. We don't want to be held responsible if he takes things any further than he already has."

Carlos stood to his feet, "Pop, you know I'm not going to touch anybody! We've already talked about this."

Mr. Bones could feel the tension in the room. On the one hand, Mr. Estrada loved his son as much as anyone could. On the other hand, the man was in a pickle. If he didn't take action... well, it wouldn't only be his son's reputation at stake.

"Carlos," Mr. Estrada said, "As much as I would love to believe you, I can't. You've let your ma and I down too many times."

"Pop, I'm not about to do something to get myself back in juvie!"

Mr. Estrada shook his head.

Mr. Bones didn't know which was worse — encouraging a judge to lock up a client or listening to a parent tell their child he had to leave the nest. Hoping to provide an alternative, he asked if the Estradas had considered homeschooling.

"We've talked about it, yes," Mr. Estrada said. "But neither one of us performed well in school. We wouldn't be qualified to teach preschool. It's not like we can afford a tutor. Right now, we're trying to locate a free placement — do you know of any military schools or boarding schools that might be able to offer him a scholarship?"

Mr. Bones felt his heartstrings being stretched out to the point they were ready to snap. The thirteen-year-old's sad eyes were getting to him. That kid didn't want to leave home. For once in his life, Mr. Bones was thankful he couldn't think of a single place to refer the family to. "Most of the facilities I'm familiar with have extensive waiting lists," he said.

Mr. Estrada sighed, "I figured as much."

A lightbulb went off. "Mr. Estrada," the probation officer said, "what if you could find someone willing to homeschool Carlos for you?"

Mr. Estrada shook his head. "Won't work. I already told you... We can't afford a tutor."

That was the exact response Mr. Bones had expected to hear. It never ceased to amaze him how the majority of society held a stronger belief in money than they did in God. "What if someone would volunteer for the position?"

Mr. Estrada shook his head again. "Nobody's going to do that — not in this day and age. Everybody has bills to pay."

The probation officer smiled, "I would."

"You would what?"

"I would tutor Carlos for you. I have mentored quite a few young men over the years, and I'd love to help out."

"Don't you have to work every day?"

"I do. But I could tutor him during non-traditional school hours. You and your wife keep him during the day and then when I get off work, I'll take care of his schooling. If we have to, we can even turn Saturdays into extra school days."

Mr. Estrada scratched his chin. "I don't know," he said. "I just don't know."

"Carlos, what do you think of the idea?" Mr. Bones asked.

"I don't care. Whatever Pop decides is fine by me... as long as it doesn't include Saturday school anyway."

13

Philip was surprised at how easy it was to get along with the school board. Letting him borrow curriculum for Carlos as opposed to making him purchase his own materials was a blessing beyond any he had expected.

Carlos was quite different than the other young men Philip had worked with in the past. So different, as a matter of fact, that the probation officer wasn't quite comfortable with him. He decided their first one-on-one time together should occur in a public place.

"Have a seat," he said as he set a pile of books on an older picnic table decorated with names, initials, and inappropriate carvings previous visitors had left behind.

Carlos sat down across from him.

"So, how do you feel about being homeschooled?"

The uncomfortable teen grinned, "I'm not sure. I think I'd rather be in class where I'm not the only one working."

Mr. Bones chuckled, "I can understand that, I suppose. But if you don't want to be shipped off to military school, it looks like this is your only option."

"Yeah, I know."

Mr. Bones flipped a science book open. "I haven't had much time to look over your curriculum yet, so today we're going to take things kind of easy. I thought we would just do a little bit of reading and talking about what we learn. How does that sound?"

"I don't have to write anything?"

"Not today anyway."

Carlos smiled, "Maybe this homeschooling thing won't be so bad after all."

"Let's try this section on dinosaurs. I'll go ahead and read the first paragraph. 'Billions of years ago, our world came into existence by means of a cosmic explosion...'" Philip stopped. How could he, a preacher, teach something contrary to everything he believed in?

"Carlos, let me show you something." Without thinking twice about it, Mr. Bones tore the page from the boy's science book and ripped it into six smaller pieces of equal size. He stacked them one on top of another.

If he hadn't had Carlos's attention before, he did now. The boy wasn't fidgeting, playing with his pencil, or paying any attention to the other people playing or walking their dogs in the park.

"Carlos, if you clap your hands really loud, I bet these pieces of paper will all come together and form one large page again. What do you think?"

Carlos shook his head with a smirk on his face.

"Try it," Mr. Bones insisted. "As a matter of fact, smack the picnic table a few times as well. Make as much noise as you can."

Carlos laughed.

"Come on man, give it a try."

Amused with his new teacher's approach to education, Carlos clapped his hands.

"Louder," Mr. Bones said. "As hard as you can!"

The young teenager hesitated for a second before looking around to make sure no one was watching; he clapped several times and pounded the table with both hands.

"Well, there goes the big bang theory! Look at that... two forces came together and it didn't magically make anything productive!"

Chuckling, Carlos countered, "But that was my hands — not gasses."

Mr. Bones grinned. "So, Carlos... do you want to experiment with gasses? What if we take some helium and find a way to mix it with propane? Do you think that will put these pieces of paper back together, give them the ability to think for themselves, give them a heart that can beat and a brain that can think?"

It was obvious Carlos had never had a teacher speak to him in such a manner. He giggled but didn't speak.

"Well?" Mr. Bones asked.

Continuing to laugh, Carlos replied, "Mr. Bones, it doesn't work like that. It was something that just happened one time!"

The probation officer shook his head. "Do you always believe everything you're told?"

"No," Carlos said, shaking his head, "but this is science. It's a proven fact."

Mr. Bones had graduated from the public school system himself. For whatever reason, it didn't bother him when he was taught about evolution... but he was at a point in his life where he knew better. The fact that kids were being brainwashed into believing lies was getting on his last nerve. "I hate to tell you this, bud, but just because something has the label of science on it doesn't mean it's accurate. Take ulcers, for example. For years science taught us that ulcers were caused by stress and poor diets. Now, we know they're caused by bacteria. Scientists used to insist the world was flat. Now we know it's round. Science considered Pluto a full planet; now they say it's only a dwarf planet."

The boy's smile faded. Instead of continuing to have an interest in what he was hearing, he went on the defensive. "You don't know what you're talking about, Mr. Bones. All of my teachers have taught me about evolution. All of them can't be wrong!"

Mr. Bones shook his head, "You would be surprised how often popular opinion turns out to be false, my friend. But let's not spend all day on this. Let's move on to something else. Before we meet tomorrow, I'm going to see if I can get my hands on a Christian-based science book. I can't teach something that contradicts the Word of God."

"How does science contradict the Bible?"

"The scriptures tell us God created man in His own image from the dust of the ground, Carlos. If science says man was created by a cosmic explosion and everything was formed from nothing... that doesn't line up."

"The Bible is not a science book. It wasn't written by Scientists. I don't have to believe anything it says."

"A lot of people don't, Carlos, but your words are pretty interesting there."

"What do you mean?"

Mr. Bones was glad the young man asked. He had no intentions of holding anything back. "You said you don't have to *believe* the Bible. I'm telling you I don't *believe* what your science books are saying. Do you realize a lot of so-called science is nothing more than a belief system?... I *believe*, for example, that God created man. Scientists *believe* a big bang created man. See how those are similar? Evolution is a theory; it has never been proven as a fact. Yet it's taught in schools as if it's the only possibility of how we came into existence."

"Evolution's a theory? How so?"

Mr. Bones was shocked to even hear such a question. "A theory is something that has not been proven. It's when people make educated guesses on a matter, but far too often their theories are later proven—"

"Hey Carlos!" a boy called, interrupting their lesson as he approached the picnic table.

"Hey, Alan," Carlos replied.

As Alan got closer, he said, "You've got guts, kid! Everybody's talking about your underwear prank! I can't believe you did that!"

Philip shook his head.

"Is this your dad?"

"No, he's my..."

Mr. Bones stood from the table, "I'm his probation officer and I would suggest you move on. Carlos will not be returning to school. The legal system nor his parents find any humor in his actions; I would highly recommend you not follow in his footsteps."

Alan shrugged his shoulders and walked away.

Perhaps meeting in a park wasn't such a great plan after all.

14

Being a juvenile probation officer was anything but a dull way of earning a living. After spending forty-five minutes in court, drug testing a probationer, getting shouted at by a belligerent grandfather, and searching for a runaway, Philip received a phone call from Mr. Estrada, asking a rather unique favor. Carlos came down with a 103-degree temperature. Mr. Estrada had a job interview to get to, and his wife's mother was on her way to the emergency room with a potential heart attack. "We called the pediatrician a few minutes ago and they said they can fit him in if we can find a way to get him there within the next half an hour or so."

Philip took a deep breath. If Carlos had a fever and he put the boy in his car, he was sure to catch whatever it was he had. But it would be selfish not to help. "Sure. I'll be right over," he said.

Mr. Estrada and Carlos met him in the driveway. "Listen, I'm in a huge rush," Mr. Estrada said. "Carlos can tell you how to get there… The doctor he normally sees is booked this afternoon, but another physician recently joined the practice and has agreed to look him over. They're expecting you."

Carlos was pale, his hair was saturated with sweat, and he was walking hunched over, holding his stomach. Philip opened the back of the car, rolled the windows down, and told Carlos to sit in the back.

By the time they arrived at the doctor's office, the boy was beginning to turn a light shade of green. "Hi Carlos," the lady in the front office said as they walked in. "Your pop says you're not feeling very well."

Carlos shook his head.

"Why don't you have a seat and I'll see if Ms. Kingston is ready for you?"

As soon as the gentlemen made their way into a couple of empty chairs, Carlos used the oldest trick in the book — the puppy-dog eyes routine, "You're coming back with me, right?"

The probation officer didn't want to. He hated doctors. But the teenager was already sick, away from his parents, and he didn't even know the pediatrician he was going to be seeing. "Sure, buddy. If you want me to."

"Thank you," Carlos said, leaning his head against the back of the seat.

A few minutes passed before a nurse made her way into the lobby. "Carlos, come on back," she said with a smile.

Philip walked him to the door.

"And who is this handsome fella you brought with you today?" the nurse asked.

"My probation officer."

"Your probation officer? You're on probation? Carlos! I can't believe you." The lady smiled, "Hi, I'm Patricia."

"I'm Philip."

"Nice to meet you. If you guys wouldn't mind, please go through the second door on your right."

Once in the room, the nurse closed the door behind them. "Carlos, hop up on the bed for me. I need to take your temperature."

Carlos complied quietly.

As the nurse took out her thermometer, she made small talk, hoping to put him more at ease, "So, Carlos... do you have a girlfriend?"

He shook his head.

"How about your probation officer? Is he seeing anybody?"

Philip felt his face turning red. Was there a neon sign above his head that said, "Girls, I'm available"?

Before Carlos had a chance to answer, Philip said, "Actually, I recently came out of a serious relationship. I'm not looking for anybody right now."

"Oh, I see. Just so you know, I wasn't asking for myself; I'm taken. But the new doctor—"

Someone tapped on the door and opened it a second later. Philip couldn't believe his eyes. "Kelly?"

"Mr. Bones? What on earth are you doing here?"

"It's a long story, but Carlos is one of my clients and his folks asked me to bring him in... What about you? You don't live around here... Are you commuting this far for work?"

"No, I accepted a new position and moved into town last week."

"Well, how about that?" Philip said.

Carlos cleared his throat to remind them he was the patient who needed cared for.

The nurse left the room with a sneaky smile on her face, winking at Kelly on her way out.

Kelly pretended not to notice. "Let's have a look at you, Carlos," she said. "I want you to pretend you're a killer whale getting ready to swallow a submarine. I need you to open that mouth so wide it feels like your jaws are coming unhinged."

Carlos smiled with his eyes as he opened wide.

Kelly checked his lungs, looked in his ears with a cone-shaped light, asked several questions, and scribbled down some notes. "I'll be back in a minute," she said.

"Thanks," Philip replied.

As she left, Carlos grinned, "You like her, don't you?"

"I do not," Mr. Bones protested.

"Really?... Tell me one thing you don't like about her then."

Mr. Bones stood and looked out the window. "There sure is a lot of traffic out there today."

"You're changing the subject," Carlos said. "You can't think of one, can you?"

"One, what?" Mr. Bones asked.

"You know what I'm talking about. Why can't you just admit you like her?"

"I don't know what you're talking about."

Kelly tapped on the door again before coming in. "Okay, little man, it looks like you caught a little stomach bug that's been crawling around. At first, I thought it might be the flu, but the swab came back negative. Be thankful!"

"Does he need antibiotics or anything?" Philip asked.

"No. If it were me, I'd just pick up something over-the-counter. It'll save you some money and get him feeling better in no time. I will have some instructions written up and will get them to you before you leave."

"Thanks, Doctor," Philip said with a hint of flirtatiousness in his voice. Where that came from, he didn't know. Yes, she was attractive but no, he wasn't interested. Or was he?

Kelly smiled, "Please don't call me that. Kelly will do just fine. Uh... Mr. Bones... do you bring your clients here very often?"

Philip grinned. "No, this is a first actually. And if you want me to call you Kelly, please knock off the whole Mr. Bones bit. My name's Philip"

"If you insist, Philip. Hey, I'm planning on coming by your office Friday to take Aunt Rose out to lunch. Think I'll see you then?"

Philip had mixed feelings about that idea. A part of him hoped to see her again that soon. Perhaps seeing more of her would help him better determine whether or not he had feelings for her. But another relationship that was destined to fail? He still hadn't figured out how to juggle his schedule any better than he had when he was with Cassie. He couldn't expect any girl to put up with his hectic lifestyle. Shrugging his shoulders, Philip said, "I don't have my calendar in front of me. I'm not sure if I'll be in the office or not. I keep a pretty busy schedule."

"I know the feeling—"

Carlos cleared his throat again, "I'm not feeling very good... Can we leave now?"

"Absolutely," Kelly replied. "Philip, tell the Estradas Carlos needs to go straight to bed when he gets home."

"They're not going to be home," Carlos interjected.

"They're not? So, where are you going when you leave here?"

"I don't know."

Kelly looked at Philip.

"I hadn't really thought about it," Philip told her. "I suppose we're just going to have to kill some time somewhere."

"Well," Kelly said, dragging out the word with a playful smile. "I get off work in twenty minutes. I don't really know anybody in town myself. We could—"

Philip shook his head. "I appreciate the offer, Kelly. But right now, I need to tend to Carlos. Maybe we'll get a chance to talk again soon, okay?"

15

Using his probation officer's suit jacket as a blanket while curling up on the floor of the office was not quite how Carlos thought they were going to kill time. Mr. Bones wouldn't let him get up or even talk for that matter.

"When are they coming to get me?" he whined after two hours of fighting his sleep.

The phone rang. "Philip Bones speaking... The doctor said he just has a stomach virus and needs a lot of rest... Oh, no. I'm sorry to hear that. Is there anything I can do... okay... um... sure... Seriously, it's no problem whatsoever. Okay... we'll head that direction now."

"Was that Pop?" Carlos asked.

It was indeed, but the man hadn't given the probation officer the kind of news that was going to overwhelm the boy with excitement. "Yeah, bud," he said. "Sounds like your grandma's being admitted to the hospital. Your parents are going to stay with her for a while just in case she needs them for anything."

Carlos was upset. It seemed everybody was more important than he was. He was sick. His grandma was sick. But his parents preferred to spend time with her. She didn't even live with them for crying out loud! "So, what am I supposed to do? Continue laying here until they decide to come get me?"

"No, bud," Philip replied. "Your pop thinks it would be best if I take you to your place. He said you know where the extra key is."

The boy's eyes widened in disbelief. Not only did his parents not want to care for him when he needed them most, but they were going to leave him home alone? If his temperature got too high, he could die! If he tried to get the rest his pediatrician said he needed, a burglar could come in on him and he might not even know they were in the house. He didn't like that idea at all! "They expect me to stay home by myself while I'm sick?"

Mr. Bones grinned. "No, buddy. I'm going to be staying with you."

"At my house?"

"Yes, sir," he said.

Carlos stood up and handed Mr. Bones his suit coat. Like his probation officer, the boy was not comfortable being alone with a man he knew so little about. It was odd enough being in the car with him and spending alone time with him at the office, but at his house? Oh, well. It wasn't like his opinion mattered anyway.

As they started for the door, Carlos whined, "I'm going to throw up!" Covering his mouth with both hands, he rushed down the hall toward the restroom.

Mr. Bones only hoped the boy made it to the toilet. The one thing he didn't have was a strong stomach, and there was no way he would be able to clean up vomit without getting ill himself. Cautiously, he made his way to the restroom and tapped on the door, "Everything okay?"

Carlos answered in a groan, "No. I threw up."

Mr. Bones cracked the door. "Did you make it to the toilet?"

"Yeah."

Walking in, Mr. Bones found his client kneeling in front of the toilet with tears streaming down his face. "Why do I always have to get sick?" the boy sniffled. "I hate this."

Mr. Bones placed an arm around him, "I know, man. Nobody likes to be sick... Let's just sit here until your stomach settles a bit before we head over to your place. I doubt either of us wants you to get sick in the car, right?"

Carlos shook his head, "I don't want to be sick anywhere."

Patting his head, the probation officer assured him everything was going to be okay.

Within an hour, the two made it to the Estrada house. Feeling sympathy for Carlos, Philip tucked him into bed and asked if there was anything he could do for him.

Using as frail of a voice as he could muster, Carlos asked, "Can you read to me?"

Mr. Bones had already been asking himself what he was going to do while the boy was in bed. He wasn't comfortable in the house. It felt odd to flip on somebody else's TV or to help himself to the fridge. Reading would pass the time of day if nothing else. "I guess I can do that," he said. "Where are your books?"

Carlos attempted to hide his half-grin, "Most of them are downstairs, but I picked a few up from the library the other day. They're on my dresser."

Mr. Bones walked over and picked up the stack. "Let's see here… We have *Revenge Fires Back*, *Shady Valentine,* and *Hidden in Harmony*. Which one do you prefer?"

"I don't know. Let me see them," Carlos said in a whiny voice.

Mr. Bones handed him the stack and waited patiently as the boy glanced at each cover and read over the descriptions. Eventually he said, "This one," holding up one wrapped in a creepy cover.

"I don't know," Mr. Bones told him. "*Shady Valentine* looks a bit eerie. You sure you're up for something like this?"

"Yeah," Carlos said. "It'll take my mind off being sick."

Mr. Bones opened to the first page and began reading, "Terror cloaked the young man's face, even though it was half-concealed by duct tape. He was anything but the typical, cooperative victim who would agree to anything to save his worthless flesh. Rocking the attractive dining chair, desperately attempting to free himself, the poor guy fell over on his side. I couldn't help but chuckle at his pitiful groan. Sauntering over, I ripped a piece of duct tape from his lips. 'Where are the valuables?' I demanded for the fifth time."

The probation officer closed the novel.

Carlos was annoyed. The book was getting off to a good start. He wondered what was going to happen to the guy who was trying to free himself. He had a feeling things were about to turn ugly. "Why'd you stop?"

"Carlos, I see too many kids who are influenced by what they read; I don't want this kind of garbage to corrupt your mind."

"It won't!" Carlos insisted. "I know the difference between what's real and what's not. Come on, Mr. Bones, please keep reading."

Mr. Bones scratched his head. Tossing the book back to the dresser, he picked up *Revenge Fires Back.* "Let's try this one instead," he said, flipping it open.

Carlos wasn't impressed. "Come on, Mr. Bones. Please? You can read that one later. After I'm asleep if you want to. I want to know what happens next in the other book you were reading to me."

"Carlos, it's either *Revenge Fires Back* or nothing. I cannot read *Shady Valentine* to you — not with a clean conscience. So, what's it going to be? Do you want to try this one or just lay here and fall asleep in silence?"

The sickling shook his head. He thrived on horror stories. Was it seriously too much to ask to have one read to him while he wasn't feeling good? Perhaps he should just tell his probation officer to leave the room so he could read *Shady Valentine* on his own. He would if he felt better. But he didn't want to read. He wanted to be read to. "Fine," he said. "Read *Revenge Backfires* or whatever it's called.

Mr. Bones chuckled. "It's *Revenge Fires Back.* Okay, here we go. 'Lightning-fashioned strobe lights presented eerie shadow monsters creeping across the Clark's tent. The frightening show was intensified by earsplitting crashes of thunder which rattled the ground beneath them.'"

Even though the novel sounded like it too could be a tad on the scary side, Mr. Bones decided it was much more appropriate than the first one the boy had requested. He read the first four chapters before his little buddy finally drifted off to sleep.

Mr. Bones went out to the living room and crashed on the couch, where he stayed until his cell phone rang at 8:00 the next morning. He glanced at the caller id. "Oh, man. How could

I have overslept?" He picked up the phone, "Good morning, Rose."

"Philip, I got worried when you didn't show up at the office. Is everything okay?"

Philip yawned, "Yeah, Rose. Carlos Estrada's parents had an emergency to deal with last night and Carlos isn't feeling very well."

"You didn't take another client to your house?"

"No... I slept at the Estrada's place."

"And you're still there now?"

Philip was tired of getting the third degree from his secretary. It wasn't just her; it was everybody. They acted like he was in the wrong every time he went out on a limb to aid one of his clients. "Yes," Philip told her. "I haven't heard from the Estrada's. I don't know if I'll make it to work today or not."

"Philip, you have appointments."

"You're going to have to reschedule them, Rose. That's all I know to tell you."

Rose sighed. "Philip, please be careful. You're going to get yourself in trouble."

"I'm a big boy, Rose. I can take care of myself."

"Okay. Call me later and let me know if you're coming in."

"Will do, Rose. Thanks for understanding."

"I didn't say I understand," Rose retorted. "I'll talk to you later."

Philip put the phone down. Sometimes he didn't know if he even understood himself. He could get fired just like anybody else could. He wasn't above the law. Rose was right — he was missing a lot of work, and he was walking on thin ice. He could have spent hours beating himself up over it, but instead he decided to check on Carlos.

When he got to the teenager's bedroom, he was shocked to find him sitting up with a laptop sitting next to him. He was even more shocked to realize Carlos had swiped the laptop from him while he was asleep. With his face coloring, the boy quickly folded down the screen.

"I see you're feeling better," Mr. Bones said.

"A little."

Mr. Bones took the laptop, "And I see you're good with computers."

Carlos grinned, "I guess you could say that."

Mr. Bones sat on the edge of the bed and reopened his computer. Just as he thought, Carlos was looking at pornography.

16

The scowl on Rose's face was fierce. "The chief wants to see you in his office," she said.

Philip should have known. "When?"

"He said he would be waiting, so I'm assuming he wants you over there right now."

Rolling his eyes, Philip headed toward Brett's office. After practically groveling at Mr. Estrada's feet for not password-protecting his laptop, he was definitely not in the mood for receiving a lecture from his boss. At least, he hoped that's all Brett planned to do.

The door was open, so Philip walked in. "You wanted to see me, sir?"

Brett's face was stone-cold. Being a former body-builder, he was not the type of guy anyone wanted to cross. "Shut the door behind you and take a seat, Philip," he growled.

The probation officer knew he was in trouble. The second he was in his chair, Brett lit into him. "I've received multiple reports regarding some questionable practices you've been engaging in. Philip, I'm not big on micromanaging, but I have the responsibility of keeping our clients as well as our department safe. What do you have to say for yourself?"

What could he say? Philip understood why Rose didn't think he should miss work to care for his clients off of the clock. He assumed the other complaint, if there was only one, came from Cassie. That too was understandable. But Brett surely knew the two had broken up. With that knowledge, it would be foolish to put stock in any allegations she may have made against him. "What questionable behaviors are you referring to, sir?" Philip asked.

"Taking a boy to an island with you, letting another one move into your home, sleeping over at a third teenager's house... Philip, do you have any idea how distasteful this looks?"

Philip took a deep breath. There was a lot he could have said just then, but a Bible verse about soft answers turning away wrath came to his mind. "Yes, sir," he replied.

"What are you going to do about it?"

That was a tough one! Where was that emergency phone call when he needed one? Couldn't Rose come tap on the door and say a client had stopped in to see him?

Brett crossed his arms and leaned back in his chair while awaiting the answer Philip didn't know how to give.

Philip was at a loss for words. He firmly believed in what he was doing and saw no reason to change his ways. However, he needed an income to survive. Not only that but if he lost his position as a juvenile probation officer, whoever replaced him might not have the same heart for at-risk youth. He hated the thoughts of young people being behind bars when they could be rehabilitated through tough love.

"Brett," he finally spit out. "I adore my job. I know I get carried away with it sometimes. It's because my heart goes out to these kids and I want to make a difference in their lives. I'm not hurting any of them. If you would like me to give you the contact information of every young man I have mentored, I would be happy to do that. You can speak with the guys and their parents. I have nothing to hide."

"Philip, I'll be honest with you here. I can't control what you do when you're not at work. However, I must say I'm not comfortable with any of our employees taking clients to remote areas or out of the public eye for mentoring purposes."

"I understand that sir," Philip said.

Brett didn't get his job by being stupid. "That doesn't mean you're going to stop mentoring, does it?"

The probation officer shook his head in silence.

"Philip, you know it will only take one allegation to ruin your career?"

"Yes, sir. I'm aware of that."

"If you're willing to take that kind of a risk, it's up to you. But don't drag the department down with you. You better make it crystal clear to any juveniles you mentor as well as to their families that you are not acting within the scope of your job. If you come under investigation, it is all on you. The department has nothing to do with this. Is that understood?"

"Yes, sir," Philip said.

"And I don't want you missing any more work on account of these young men."

"Understood."

"Good... You can get back to your work now," Brett said.

The meeting went better than Philip thought it would, although it gave him a lot to think about. Sure, he already knew what the risks were, but somehow hearing it from his superior made it more real. If one person accused him of doing something wrong, he could be banned from working with young people for life. He had heard horror stories of such things, but surely it would never happen to him.

As he passed Rose's desk, she asked, "How did that go?"

Philip shook his head, "I don't feel like talking about it right now, Rose... Did I get any messages?"

"Only one," she replied. "Tamara Andrews said she would appreciate it if you could give her a call regarding her son, Billy."

"Great," Philip said. "I hope he's not violated his probation again... I'll give her a call. Thanks, Rose."

Billy, Billy, Billy. When was that boy ever going to learn? Philip didn't even want to make the phone call to find out. The way his day was going, he wouldn't be surprised to find out the boy had been locked up for stealing a police cruiser.

"Hello?" Tamara answered.

"Tamara, this is Mr. Bones. My secretary said you needed to speak with me?"

"I did. It's about Billy. You won't believe what that boy's gone and done now."

The probation officer had a few guesses. It wouldn't be very professional to say any of them out loud. Even if it was, it probably wouldn't fly very well with Tamara. "I'm afraid to ask," he said.

"He just brought home his progress report. Does that give you any idea?"

Philip shook his head. How could the kid's grades have slipped again so soon? He pictured a progress report with a grade point average of 0.50. Surely it was better than that. "How bad was it?" he asked.

"Guess how many F's he got, Mr. Bones."

Philip assumed the worst. If she was taking the time to call him, he assumed he must have flunked every class. He had to

84

be optimistic — or at least pretend to be. "Let's see," he said. "Billy has seven classes per day so I'd guess... five?"

Tamara giggled, "Zero! As a matter of fact, he only got one D. All the rest were B's and C's. I can't believe it! He hasn't gotten good grades like this since he was in third grade. You've given me my son back!"

Philip grinned. Finally, some good news. "Is Billy around?" he asked.

"Yeah, hold on and I'll get him for you."

Philip couldn't wait to speak with the kid. Especially considering the fact he still owed him one. Not long after the two had met, Billy got him all fired up by pretending he had been skipping school. It was time for the long-awaited payback.

"Hey, Mr. Bones? Momma tell ya the good news?" he asked, picking up the line."

"She did, Billy," Mr. Bones said in a serious tone of voice. "But that's not what I wanted to speak with you about."

"What's up then?"

Oh, this was going to be fun! The probation officer only wished there was a way he could see the teenager's facial expressions. The hair on the back of that boy's neck was about to stand straight on end. "Billy, do you remember when you and I had a talk about the importance of keeping yourself pure until you're an adult?"

"Yes, sir. But I told you it was too late for that kinda talk."

"I remember. But there's a problem, Billy."

"What kind of problem?"

"The prosecutor got in touch with me a little while ago. It seems a young lady's parents have contacted their office claiming their daughter is pregnant and she got that way because you forced yourself on her. The police are on their way—"

"What? I ain't force myself on nobody! What Keisha be thinkin'? I ain't gonna be no daddy, and I most certainly ain't do nothin' against her will!"

Mr. Bones thought about letting it go, but it was too soon. He had to take it a step further. "You'll just have to explain that to the investigator when he stops by."

"The investigator? What you talkin' about? They comin' here to arrest me?"

Philip couldn't take it anymore. He burst into a fit of laughter. "Got you, boy!"

"What?"

"Remember when you got me all riled up about you skipping school? I told you I'd get you back."

"That was a long time ago!"

"It was. I had to wait until I knew you wouldn't be expecting anything."

Billy wasn't amused. "Funny," he said. "Real funny."

17

As if Philip's day hadn't already been a colossal roller coaster, did he really hear her voice in the lobby?

"What's this?" he heard Rose ask.

"I made it for Philip. Is he here?"

Rose giggled, "He sure is. Let me get him for you."

Seconds later, Rose tapped on the door and peeked her head through. "Philip, can you come out here for a minute?"

"Rose? I told you I'm not into the whole matchmaking thing."

"Philip... don't be rude. Kelly brought you something. At least come out here and accept it in person."

Philip stood and followed Rose out to the lobby. Kelly reached a pie out toward him. "Hope you like apple," she said.

Even though the probation officer wasn't looking for a girlfriend, his mouth was already watering over that apple pie. He couldn't mask his delight. "My favorite," he said. "How did you know?"

"Just a hunch," she said. "How's Carlos doing?"

Philip was surprised she remembered the boy's name. "He's doing better. Thanks for asking."

"I'm glad to hear that. But hey, I just came back to take my aunt out to dinner. We were going to do lunch but I've had a crazy day."

Philip chuckled.

"What's so funny?" Kelly asked.

"At least I'm not the only one. Sometimes I wish I could go to bed and start all over."

Kelly smiled, "You know... if you ever need anybody to talk to, I'm available... not like available, available, but... you know what I mean, right?"

Philip couldn't help but laugh as he watched Kelly blush. "Yeah, I know what you mean. I'll think about taking you up on that offer. But let's not rush into anything."

"Deal," she said. "But I guess we better be going."

"No problem," Philip replied. "Thanks again for the pie."

"You're welcome," she said before leaving the office with her aunt.

Philip brought the pie up to his nose and smelled its sweet aroma as he returned to his office. It just so happened that he had some plastic silverware in his drawer, and who needed a plate? He could eat it right out of the tin!

As he opened his drawer, his cell phone rang. "Philip Bones speaking."

"Hey, preacher boy," a familiar voice said.

"Preacher boy?" Philip chuckled. "Who is this?"

"Lisa... Brother Michael's daughter."

Philip smiled. What on earth did Lisa Michaels want and what prompted her to call him at work of all places? There was only one way to find out. "And how's the playdough artist doing today?"

"I can't complain," she said. "The reason I'm calling... well, first of all, do you know I'm a teacher?"

A teacher? Lisa? Philip couldn't believe it. What did she teach? Drama? Preschool maybe? He couldn't imagine her having a serious side. Then again, she did teach a class at her church, so maybe there was more to the girl than met the eye. "I had no idea," Philip replied.

"Well, I am. I teach history."

"Interesting," Philip said. "I wouldn't think you have time to teach with all of your sculpting and canine glamour shots."

Lisa giggled, "I lead a pretty exciting life, huh?"

"That you do," Philip said. There was no denying that one. He just hoped she wasn't going to drag him into some crazy scheme of hers. He suspected she was going to go ghost hunting or something and wanted him to accompany her through a haunted house. No, probably not that bad. Surely not? "What can I help you with today, Lisa?"

"Well... two weeks from Friday our school is going to hold a career day and I was wondering if you might be available to come in and tell our students a little bit about probation work?"

Philip didn't have to think twice about it. "I would count it an honor," he said. "What time do I need to be there?"

"Why don't you come by at 12:30? That way we can have lunch together before everything kicks off at 1:00. Will that work?"

That sly devil! She intentionally worded that in such a way that Philip couldn't possibly say no. Then again, he wasn't even sure if he wanted to say no. It might be interesting to talk to Lisa when she was away from her family. He wondered what she was like when she was in a slightly more professional environment. "Sure, 12:30 sounds like a plan. What school do you work at?"

"Westview Middle."

Philip chuckled. "Seriously? I have a client who attends there."

"Alden's a great kid, isn't he?" Lisa asked.

"How do you know Alden reports to me?"

"It's a small school, and the walls have ears. Especially when a cute, single probation officer's involved."

"Cute?" Philip laughed. "Is that what the walls say about me?"

"Every time you leave the building."

Lisa wasn't the only one who lived an interesting life. Philip wondered what his future was to hold. Was he destined to remain a bachelor who spent his life mentoring young men or would he find the love of his life and live happily ever after with her?

18

The binoculars gave Carlos just the view he needed. Beth was working out in her backyard. That girl was something else! His eyes widened and he grinned from ear to ear as the sixteen-year-old continued her set of squats. Carlos didn't care that Beth wanted nothing to do with him. Checking her out from next-door was good enough!

Her father came out on the porch and motioned for her to come inside. The show was over! Carlos moved his binoculars around, hoping to find another show. He found one alright — Mrs. Davenport was crawling around her living room on her hands and knees, searching for something. If he were a betting person, Carlos would have bet a hundred bucks it was her keys.

The door to his bedroom burst open. "Carlos!" Ma shouted. "Where did you get those?"

The teenager smiled, "They were up in the attic."

"In the attic?... You were told to stay in your room!"

"I've been in here all afternoon."

Ma put her hands on her hips. "Then how did you get the binoculars?"

"I didn't get them today," Carlos said with a smirk. "I've had 'em for a couple of weeks."

Ma held out an open palm. Even though Carlos knew what she wanted, he gave her a five.

"This is not a time for games!" Ma shouted. "Hand them over, now!"

Smiling, Carlos placed the binoculars in her palm. His mother held them up to her face and aimed them toward the Davenport's place, trying to see what her son had been gawking at. It took her a few minutes, but she finally got them focused in. "Were you watching Mrs. Davenport?" she asked. She jerked the binoculars down and whipped the curtains closed. "See what you did, Carlos? She just saw me!"

Now that was funny! Carlos burst into a fit of laughter. He could hear it now — Ma was going to be reported as a peeping tom. Even if she was able to talk her way out of it, she was going to be humiliated. His ma never wanted anything to do with being in the limelight.

Ma wagged her finger at Carlos, "Stop laughing... get that cheesy grin off your face right now!"

How could she expect him to pretend it wasn't funny? Hopefully, she would find the humor in the situation and laugh about it later. The fire in her eye said otherwise. So did her heavy footsteps as she exited the room and slammed the door behind her.

Carlos reopened his curtains — Mrs. Davenport was nowhere in sight. Now what could he look at? Even though the neighbor's dog scattering trash all over another neighbor's yard was amusing, it wasn't quite what he was looking for.

His door burst open again. Carlos spun around to find Pop glaring at him. "I see you're not laughing anymore," he said.

Carlos shook his head.

"Your ma and I are ashamed of you, son. You get into pornography on your probation officer's computer and now this! Carlos, when are you going to learn?"

The devious young man smiled, "I'm already learning, Pop."

"What are you learning?"

"That we live in the midst of some fine creatures."

Pop was not amused. "Carlos, women are not to be drooled over. They're people — not objects."

Carlos sat on the edge of his bed. "You're just saying that because you're married, Pop. If you were my age, you know you'd be checking 'em out just like I am."

Pop stormed over to the window and jerked the curtains closed. "Don't even think about opening them any time soon! You are to stay on your bed until further notice. You can get up to use the restroom and nothing else."

"What about meals?"

"We'll bring you your food."

The hard-hearted teen let out a sigh. He enjoyed being grounded about as much as grasshoppers enjoyed lawnmowers. "How long do I have to stay on my bed, Pop?"

"We haven't decided yet."

Carlos pulled his feet up on the bed and hugged his knees. "Are you reporting this to Mr. Bones?"

"What do you think?" Pop asked.

Carlos shrugged.

Without another word, Pop stormed out of the room.

Laying on his back, Carlos looked at his four boring walls. Staying on his bed doing absolutely nothing was going to be torture. He had to do something. *Oh yeah,* he told himself. *The library books! It'd be better than just sitting here.*

There was only one problem — the books were still in their place atop his dresser. Carlos sat on his knees and stretched as far as possible, but they were completely out of reach. Putting his feet on the floor, the boy thought about standing up, but he tried to be an obedient kid — at least when he knew his pop was about ready to snap.

Taking his belt off, he flung the buckle end toward the books, hoping to snag them in such a way that he could drag them in his direction. After about a dozen misses, he realized it was time for a different plan. It's a good thing his bed had wheels on the bottom of it! Laying on his tummy, he reached down and unlocked them, one at a time.

Carlos sat up, rocked his body enough that the bed scooted a couple of centimeters forward, and rocked harder. Slowly, but surely the bed got close enough that he could easily reach the books. He smiled as he pulled the stack onto his bed.

Giving them a once-over, he knew which one he was going to read. *Shady Valentine* — if his probation officer specifically told him that's the one he would least recommend, it was probably the book Carlos would enjoy the most. Opening the cover, he began reading where Mr. Bones had left off. Arnold Valentine was one crazy excuse for a human being. Carlos was thankful he decided to read it early in the evening — if he had waited until bedtime, he probably wouldn't have been able to fall asleep.

Pop barged through the door again, phone in hand. "Carlos!" he shouted. "You're supposed to be sitting on that bed doing nothing!"

"You didn't say that, Pop," Carlos replied with a grin. "All you told me is to stay on my bed... You didn't say I couldn't read."

Pop tossed the phone on the bed and grabbed the front of his son's shirt, just below his neck. He partially lifted the thirteen-year-old off of the bed. Staring deep into his eyes, he said, "One way or another, you are going to learn to do as you're told!"

Carlos didn't dare to make a sound. For a moment, the room was silent. Then a voice could be heard coming through the phone, "Mr. Estrada?... Can you hear me?"

Releasing his son's shirt, Mr. Estrada picked up the phone. "Yes, sir... I'm here. Sorry about that," he said. "Yes, sir. Just a second."

Pop handed the phone to Carlos, "Your probation officer would like to have a word with you."

19

It was time for the bare bones approach — if nothing else was going to get the teenager's attention, the probation officer was certain this would do the trick. Mr. Bones was glad the Estradas agreed to allow him to intervene. "Okay, Carlos... here's the deal, partner... Your bedroom is about to become your private jail cell."

Carlos smirked, "It already is. What are you talking about?"

"Watch and learn, my friend... watch and learn." Mr. Bones pulled a screwdriver out of his pocket and wasted no time in taking the bedroom door off its hinges. Carlos rolled his eyes as he watched in silence from his bed.

The probation officer stepped into in the hall and brought a dolly into the room.

"What's that for?" Carlos asked.

Mr. Bones didn't answer. Instead, he loaded the dresser onto the dolly and wheeled it out of the room. Per his conversation with the boy's parents, Mr. Bones took the dresser to a storage building behind the house.

As he headed back inside, he remembered something — the novels; they weren't on the dresser. When he got to the room, he glanced around for them. "Alright, Carlos. Where are your library books?"

Carlos shrugged his shoulders.

"Where are they, Carlos?"

The teenager pulled the books out from under his pillow and handed them to Mr. Bones.

"Where's the other one?"

"What other one?"

Mr. Bones felt himself getting flustered. It didn't matter. The young man was not going to get his way, no matter what. With Carlos still sitting on his bed, the probation officer raised up his mattress. He grabbed *Shady Valentine* and said, "This one... I was just going to put these away for a little while, but since you tried to hide one from me and then play stupid, I'm going to have your parents return every last one of them to the library."

Carlos rolled his eyes again, "I haven't read them yet."

"And you're not going to! As a matter of fact—" Mr. Bones snatched his pillow, "You won't be needing this either."

By the time the probation officer was finished, the bedroom consisted of nothing but a mattress, a sheet, and a blanket. Mr. Bones put black tape on the floor outlining the mattress and told Carlos the mattress was not to be moved out of its place for any reason. "Your folks will bring you your clothes every morning. When I tutor you in the evenings, we will do that here in your room as well. You will remain grounded, having nothing in here until I say otherwise. Even then, you'll only get one item back at a time and you will not get to choose which one you get first."

If there was one thing Mr. Bones knew about teenagers, it was that they would go insane if they had nothing to do. Carlos needed to have his will broken, and the probation officer hoped with everything in him that this would accomplish his mission. If it didn't, he was afraid he might have to resort to petitioning the judge to have his probation revoked — a step he wouldn't take unless absolutely necessary.

Regardless, he had to hurry up and get home; it was Saturday evening, and he hadn't even begun preparing for his sermon.

Three blocks from the Estrada place, it started raining. Before he knew it, the rain turned to hail. Wind gusted so fiercely he could feel the pressure against the side of his car. Ahead, a vehicle was pulled to the side, and its flashers were on.

Looking closer, Mr. Bones could faintly see the outline of a woman attempting to change a flat tire. As she came into better view, he felt compassion for her. She was drenched from head to toe. It didn't appear as though she had a clue how to get the tire off.

The probation officer had no desire to step out into the storm, but he couldn't call himself a gentleman if he left the lady out there on her own. He pulled up behind the stranded motorist. It looked like she glanced at him for a second, but the hail was coming down so quickly that he wasn't one-hundred percent sure.

Jumping out of his vehicle, Philip jogged toward her, "Get back in the car!" he shouted over the wind. "Let me take care of this."

To his surprise, when the lady looked up, he recognized her — of all people, he couldn't believe it was Kelly. Her face lit up at the sight of his familiar face. "Philip!... You are such a sweetheart!"

He smiled, "Get back in the car and get that heat on. I don't want you to catch pneumonia."

"What about you?" she asked.

"I'll be fine. I've changed my fair share of tires in bad weather before. I'll have it done in no time."

As Kelly walked toward the front of the car, Philip chuckled. She had gotten the car jacked up but hadn't loosened any of the lug bolts first. He lowered the jack so the tire could rest on the ground. Picking up the wheel wrench, he loosened the lug bolts before raising the car back up. Within less than ten minutes, he had a donut tire in place and the car back on the ground.

He tapped on her window, "You're all set. I doubt you'll find any tire shops open tonight. More than likely you won't be able to find anything tomorrow either. But Monday, you'll want to get that tire patched. It's not good to drive around on a donut."

Kelly laughed. "Speaking of donuts... I insist on buying you a couple as a way of saying thank you."

"You already baked me an—"

Kelly was not the kind to take no for an answer. She cut him off, "Follow me down to Gretchen's Bakery. I could use a donut or two myself."

Philip chuckled, "I'll follow you, but only if you let me treat you."

"We'll see about that," she said while pulling out.

Philip scratched his head as he watched her drive away. Whether he wanted to admit it or not, he liked her sense of style. Rushing back to his car, he jumped in and sped toward the bakery.

By the time he got inside, Kelly was already sitting at a table with a dozen donuts and two bottles of milk. "I picked up a variety," she said. "I'm sure you can at least find a few in here that you like."

Philip shook his head. "You shouldn't have," he said.

"But I did."

"Shall we pray?"

Kelly nodded before bowing her head and waiting.

"Heavenly Father, we would like to thank You for this opportunity to come before Your throne. We appreciate Your protection, and the time You're giving us to fellowship with one another this evening. Lord, please bless this food that we're about to eat. In Jesus's name we pray, Amen."

As they looked up, Kelly giggled.

"What?" Philip asked with a slight chuckle.

"Sorry," she said. "I was waiting for you to ask God to help these donuts nourish our bodies. I'm so glad you didn't... I'd have laughed for sure."

20

Carlos was tired of repeatedly counting the same ceiling fan blades, taking cat naps, and punching his mattress. "Can I please come out now?" he asked his ma.

"No, sir. You will not be ungrounded until your probation officer says so!"

Carlos gave her puppy-dog eyes, "But Ma... you and Pop are my parents — not him... Please?"

Putting a finger to her lips, Ma shook her head and backed out of the room.

"Please, Ma! At least stay in here and keep me company! I'm bored!"

Again, she shook her head and walked away.

The bored teenager didn't know how much more he could take. He needed people to talk to, things to do... at least a change of scenery once in a while. Burying his face in his mattress, Carlos sulked for half an hour before finally falling asleep.

He didn't wake up until his ma gently shook him. "Your probation officer's on his way."

Carlos rubbed his eyes. "What's he coming over for?"

"For homeschooling, remember?"

For a whole ten seconds, the young man had hope. His face lit up, "Are we going to the park again?"

"Funny," Ma said. "You'll do your schooling right here."

Carlos turned his head away from her. His ma quietly left the room. It was then that Carlos decided he had no choice but to up his game. He had to gain the upper hand — no matter what it took.

Getting the feeling he was going to be locked in his room until he had gray hair, the young man decided being good wasn't the way to go. He had to discourage his probation officer from tutoring him. If he could succeed, his parents would have to place him back in public school. If nothing else, that would at least get him out of his room for several hours a day.

It wasn't long before Mr. Bones knocked on the door frame.

"Come in," Carlos said.

Mr. Bones carried a chair into the room and set it down next to the boy's mattress. "Good afternoon," he said.

"Afternoon," Carlos replied.

"I picked up some new books this afternoon. I believe you'll really enjoy—"

"How long do I have to stay in my *private prison cell*?" Carlos interrupted.

Mr. Bones chose to ignore the question. Handing Carlos a small book, he said, "Let's begin with math."

The not-so-happy student shoved the book away without as much as looking at the cover. "Why did you volunteer to teach me?"

"Because I care about you and want to help you with your future."

Carlos figured that was the truth, but he wasn't about to let his probation officer know that. He was going to make the man feel like a criminal. Like the scum on the bottom of his shoe. By the time this tutoring session was over, Mr. Bones was not going to want to step foot in his house ever again. "You and I both know the reason you're volunteering, and it has nothing to do with my future."

The probation officer was confused. He sensed something was up but couldn't quite place his finger on what it was. "What do you mean?" he asked.

Carlos was glad he asked. But Mr. Bones wasn't going to like the answer! "I've been giving this some thought. You didn't ask if you could become my teacher until after you saw me at school that day. You know, when I was in my underwear... You were watching me from the other end of the hallway. You volunteered to walk me down to the office. At first, I thought you were just being a jerk. You know, doing your job. Trying to get me in trouble. But as I got to thinking, I realized that's not what you were doing at all. You wanted to walk with a boy who was practically naked, didn't you? That's when you decided—"

"Carlos!" Mr. Bones snapped. "How dare you say such a thing!"

Little did he know, the boy was only beginning. "You're pretty quick, Mr. Bones. First, you take me out to the park to make it look like you weren't going to try anything. And now we're up here together in my bedroom. Just me and you. Nobody around. What are you planning on doing to me?"

Mr. Bones stood up. "Carlos, stop! That's enough!"

Carlos didn't feel like stopping — not until he got his way. Mr. Bones was a stubborn guy. Idle words might not be enough to stop him. It was time to take things to a whole new level.

Standing up on his mattress, he unfastened his jeans and dropped them to his ankles. "Is this what you wanted to see?"

"Pull those pants up, now!" Mr. Bones demanded.

Carlos placed both hands behind his head and shook his hips. "This is what you wanted to be alone with me for, isn't it? How many other boys have you done this to, Mr. Bones?"

Scared out of his mind, the probation officer stepped into the hallway. "Mr. Estrada!" he shouted. "Can you come up here for a moment?"

Carlos jerked his pants back up, laid on his mattress, and opened his new math book. "I'm going to deny everything," he whispered loudly.

The probation officer shook his head. A minute or so passed before Pop made his way to the room. "What's going on?" he asked.

"Your son is acting out inappropriately again," Mr. Bones replied. "He accused me of being a pedophile. Claimed I wasn't interested in helping him until I saw him in his underwear at school. He dropped his—"

"Mr. Bones?" Carlos spoke in a surprised tone. "I've been laying right here the whole time... Oh, I get it! You're upset because you asked me to model my superhero costume again and I didn't go along with you... Now, you're trying to turn the tables on me, so Pop doesn't report you to the police."

The probation officer's face turned red. "Mr. Estrada," he said, "I asked you to come up here in order to protect my reputation. I have no desire to see your son at any time when he is not fully clothed; I hope you know that."

"Mr. Bones," Pop said, "I need a few minutes alone with my son. Would you mind waiting in the living room?"

"No problem," the probation officer said. He left the room as white as a ghost.

Once Mr. Bones was out of earshot, Pop said, "Carlos, I want you to shoot straight with me. Allegations like the one you just made are quite serious. If Mr. Bones really—"

"He did, Pa! I didn't make it up!"

"Let me finish, Carlos — if your probation officer asked you to show him your superhero costume, he could be arrested. He would never be allowed to work with juveniles again. He would lose his job and may not even be able to preach any longer... If he did something wrong, he deserves all of that and then some. But if he didn't and you're making this up, you could ruin an innocent man's entire life. Now tell me the truth. What happened in here?"

Carlos flipped through his math book, trying to stall any way he could.

"Carlos?"

The boy continued turning pages until his father jerked the book out of his hand.

Looking up, Carlos said, "I wasn't trying to ruin anybody's life. I just wanted to go back to public school."

"So, Mr. Bones was telling the truth? You made all of this up?"

Carlos nodded nervously.

"You are not going to return to public school — no matter what! I just hope your probation officer is willing to continue working with you. Wait here... I'll be back in a minute."

The boy's chest tightened. Carlos couldn't believe he had stooped so low. Nor could he believe he had gotten cold feet and told the truth. His probation officer was probably boiling. He couldn't blame the man.

Pop escorted Mr. Bones into the room, "I believe my boy has something he needs to say to you," he said, glaring at Carlos.

"I'm sorry," the teenager lied. "I wasn't thinking."

"Oh, you were thinking alright," Mr. Bones replied. "But your thought process was wicked. I couldn't be more ashamed of you."

"Pop says I can't go back to public school."

"No, you can't, Carlos," Mr. Bones agreed.

"Are you going to continue teaching me?"

"I don't know, Carlos. An accusation like the one you made against me could have consequences that last a lifetime. I don't know that I'm willing to take that kind of a chance."

Carlos grinned. "I guess that settles it, Pop. If he won't teach me and I can't go to public school, I guess I'll just have to drop out."

Mr. Bones responded before Pop could say a word. "I didn't say I won't teach you. I said I don't know if I will. I need some time to think and pray about this situation."

21

Studying for his sermon was a struggle. All Philip could think about was the allegation Carlos had made against him. Perhaps everyone was right — going the extra mile to help troubled youths wasn't worth the risk. Maybe it was time to cut out the volunteer work. It was obviously going to burn his behind.

Across the page from where he was studying, a verse popped out at him. Proverbs 29:25 read "The fear of man bringeth a snare: but whoso putteth his trust in the LORD shall be safe."

Philip closed his eyes, "Do you know how hard this is, God? To not be afraid of man? I feel like the opposite of this verse is true. If I don't have a reasonable fear of my clients, I'm going to fall right into a trap. I don't want to put my entire career at stake—"

He looked at the verse a second time. "I know you're right, God. You called me to work with these young men. You'll protect me. I just have to put my faith in you."

No matter how hard he tried, Philip couldn't bring himself to study for the message he was supposed to preach the following evening. Instead, he searched the scriptures for passages that might help him with his dilemma.

Forty-five minutes into his study, the phone rang. It was Mr. Estrada. "Sorry to bother you, Mr. Bones, but Carlos wants to know if he can speak with you."

Philip smiled, curious as to how God might have worked on the young man's heart. "Sure, put him on."

"Hi, Mr. Bones," he began. "I... um... wanted to apologize again. I know I really messed up yesterday."

That was the understatement of the century. Still, the probation officer appreciated the apology. "You did indeed," he said.

Carlos didn't seem to care that Mr. Bones didn't say he forgave him. He just moved right along, "Have you made a decision yet about whether or not you'll continue teaching me?"

Mr. Bones answered the question with one of his own, "Do you want me to?"

There was a brief pause, followed by a quiet, "Yes, sir."

The hesitant tone was alarming. A dead giveaway that something was amiss. "Did your pop tell you to say that?"

"Yes, sir."

"Thank you for your honesty. Carlos, here's the deal... I'm willing to continue teaching you, but we need to put some safeguards in place. You and I will never be alone together under any circumstances. We will not have physical contact of any kind. You will be required to be fully clothed any time I'm working with you. There cannot be any more allegations made—"

"I understand," Carlos said.

"Good. One final thing — before I work with you again, you need to write a paper about what you did yesterday and why you did it. I want it to be dated. Ask your pop and ma to sign as witnesses."

"Why?"

"I will not teach you until it's done. That's why."

"Yes, sir," Carlos said.

Mr. Bones glanced down at his Bible, reminding him of what day it was. Wednesdays and Sundays were non-school days, no matter what. Church came first. "I won't be coming by tomorrow," he said, "but have it done by the time I get there Thursday evening."

"Yes, sir."

"Does your pop need to speak with me?"

There was a brief silence again before a quick, "No. He doesn't need to."

"In that case, it was nice talking to you. Have a good night."

"You too, Mr. Bones."

Philip smiled, recognizing that phone call was a way for God to show him He had everything under control. The Lord wanted him to continue working with the teenager, as uncomfortable as it may be.

With that taken care of, the probation officer was finally able to return to focusing on his Wednesday evening sermon — it was going to be his last time preaching at Freedom Baptist Church as they had voted in a new pastor who would be starting the following Sunday morning.

Philip had mixed emotions about the service. A part of him was relieved that he wouldn't have to find the time to study for three sermons per week. Another part of him was going to miss it. Keeping his nose in The Book had enabled him to experience significant spiritual growth. Of course, he could continue studying that much even if he wasn't preaching — but he knew it wouldn't be the same.

As much as Philip tried not to think about her, there was also the Lisa factor. He had really enjoyed getting to know her. He still didn't know if there was any chance the two of them could ever become a couple, but it was always a possibility. If Philip returned to Clover Baptist, he and Lisa might not ever see one another again. But... if God was in it, it would happen.

Philip's phone rang again. This time it was Pastor Jahmal. "Brother Philip, how are you doing, man?"

The probation-officer-turned-preacher grinned, "Doing great, Pastor! How's everything at the church?"

"No complaints. We've been missing you, Brother. How have things been going at Freedom Baptist?"

Several thoughts immediately came to mind. He could tell him about Lisa and how difficult it was going to be to leave because of her. Then again, how immature might that sound? He could tell him about how much more comfortable he was getting with his preaching. But that could easily be misconstrued. Perhaps the less he said, the better off he would be. "Really well, Pastor. Thank you so much for giving me this opportunity."

"Don't thank me, Brother. Thank the good Lord up above... Philip, the reason I was calling is to see if you might be interested in another opportunity."

That timing couldn't have been any better. Just as one door was closing, it appeared as though another one might be getting ready to swing open. "Another opportunity? Like what?"

"You know how our teen department has been growing lately?"

"Yes, sir."

"We're up to twenty-two teenagers coming on Sunday mornings. Ms. Belinda has decided to retire. I'm thinking it might be a great time to split the class in two. We have a new lady coming now that's eager to work in the church. She has worked with youth groups at other churches and has a clean background. If you're interested, I'd like you to take the teen boys and have her take the teen girls. What do you think?"

Philip chuckled. Teens were his life. He didn't have to give the proposition a second thought. "I guess I can do that," he replied.

"I knew you would," Pastor Jahmal said. "If you don't mind, go ahead and put a message together; you can start Sunday morning."

"You got it, Pastor."

Philip's mind was already spinning — perhaps he could even talk some of his clients into coming if they knew he was going to teach — he was certain Alden and maybe even Billy would come. He would definitely send out some invitations and see if he could grow his class.

Another thought hit him — a new lady was attending the church? Maybe Lisa wasn't the right one for him. Perhaps God wanted the man to return to Clover Baptist just for that reason. Surely, he and whoever this new lady was, would work together sometimes — perhaps organize some youth activities where both the guys and the girls could do things together? He wished he would have asked more questions — like how old this lady was, where she came from, and most importantly whether or not she had a ring on her finger. Not that he was necessarily ready to start dating again or anything like that.

22

Philip hadn't as much as turned his car off before Lisa pecked on the window. The probation officer's eyes were immediately drawn to the one arm that was obviously holding something behind her back.

Opening his door, Philip asked, "What do you have there?"

Lisa grinned as she slowly pulled out a gift wrapped in camouflage paper. "I hope you like it," she said. "It's a thank you gift for preaching for us these past few weeks."

"Oh, you didn't have to do that," Philip said.

"Of course, I did. Open it, please!"

Philip smiled as he hesitantly opened the package. His eyes widened, "Playdough?... Really?"

Lisa donned a mischievous smile. "Absolutely!" she giggled. "You need to develop some new hobbies... sculpting should be right up your alley."

Philip suddenly felt something for Lisa he hadn't felt before. His face began to glow and his heart seemed to skip a few beats. Philip liked the feeling, even though he didn't understand it. "And what makes you think I would enjoy sculpting?" he asked.

"Oh, I don't know," Lisa said playfully. "Maybe so you and I can have an excuse to spend some extra time together? I'd love to meet up with you sometime so we can have a sculpting session together. What do you think?"

Philip couldn't believe his ears. What kind of proposition was that? "I, uh—"

"Wonderful!" Lisa exclaimed. "I have some time Saturday. Could we meet then?"

With a smirk on his face, Philip shook his head. "Sure. Why not?"

Lisa giggled, "How about if you come over to our place around noon? Would that work?"

"I don't see any reason why that would be a problem."

After placing his special gift in the car, Philip and Lisa walked into the church together. Mrs. Francis, an elderly widow, met them just inside the door. She glanced at Philip, then at Lisa, then back at Philip again. "Are you two...?"

"Coming into church, yes ma'am," Philip replied.

Mrs. Francis snickered, "You know what I'm talking about. You two are seeing each other, aren't you?"

"Well, our eyes are open if that's what you mean," Lisa said while winking at Philip.

"I can take a hint," Mrs. Francis replied. "I shouldn't be putting my nose where it doesn't belong."

"No problem," Philip said. "Don't worry about it."

Philip proceeded toward his pew with Lisa walking right along beside of him. Even though he felt like he may be developing a crush on her, he wanted to separate himself from her. To take things slow. It's not like they were dating or anything.

Taking a seat, he placed a hymnal next to him. Lisa eased herself down next to it. "What did you put the book here for?" she asked.

"I thought it would look better that way. Wouldn't want anybody to get the wrong idea."

"The six-inch rule, huh?"

Philip chuckled, "Yeah, something like that I suppose."

Brother Michaels came in a moment later. "Good evening," he said, placing a hand on Philip's shoulder. "We are extremely grateful for you filling in for us these past six weeks or so. You've been a real blessing."

"It's been a growing experience for me, sir."

"Pastor Jahmal tells me you're going to start working with the teens over at your home church?"

Wow! Philip couldn't believe how quickly word had already gotten around. Was there even any point in answering the question. Brother Michaels probably knew about it before he did. Social skills, it's a good thing Philip was developing them. "Yes, sir," he said. "I start Sunday morning."

"That's wonderful, man. We'll be praying that God will bless your work abundantly. But... I'll tell you this as well. I'm not one to proselytize or anything like that, but if you ever feel God leading you out of that church, we could definitely find a place for you here."

"I appreciate that," Philip replied. "But I believe Clover Baptist is where God placed me and where He intends for me to stay."

"I'm glad to hear that, Philip. But I've got to get up front. It looks like it's about time for the service to start."

Suddenly Philip felt like he wouldn't be able to preach. A knot was swelling up in his throat. He was more nervous at that moment than he had been the first time he had stood behind a pulpit.

"What's the matter?" Lisa asked.

Philip stared at the hymnal between them. The last thing he wanted to do was tell her he was getting the jitters. He would sound foolish. "Nothing," he replied.

"Philip, if something's wrong, tell me."

The preacher boy shrugged. He had no choice but to tell her. "I just have a bad case of the butterflies."

"Why? Because it's your last night here?... We're still going to see each other, Philip. You're coming over Saturday, remember?"

Lisa was getting quite good at putting Philip in odd predicaments. His anxiety had absolutely nothing to do with the girl — not this time anyway. He had enjoyed being somewhat of an interim pastor. Somehow it felt as if he were abandoning his flock — like the well-being of the congregation was his responsibility. But he couldn't tell Lisa that.

"I know," he told her. "I'm not sure what came over me."

The piano began to play and Brother Michaels asked the congregation if they could stand for their first hymn. Philip hoped a song or two might relieve some of his tension.

After the first hymn, however, Brother Michaels told the congregation they could be seated. "Church, as you all know this will be the last message we hear from Brother Bones. Sunday morning he will be assuming a new role teaching a class for teenage boys at his home church, Clover Baptist. Immediately following the service this evening, we're going to have some refreshments downstairs and will be taking up a love offering for our dear brother to show him our appreciation.

Philip was embarrassed beyond all measure. "That's not necessary, Brother Michaels. I don't need a love offering. Give it to your new pastor to help him get settled in."

Brother Michaels waved Philip down. "That, church, is exactly why we are going to do this for Philip. He's a very humble man, and we will not allow him to rob us of a blessing. Before we have him come up here to preach his final message, let's go ahead and sing another song. Please stand to your feet and let's sing page 233."

So good to the idea of calming down! Philip's palms began to sweat. It was a struggle even to get his words out. Before he knew what happened, the congregation was sitting down and it was time to approach the pulpit.

Nervously, he picked up his Bible. "You've got this," Lisa said. "You'll do great!"

With a half-hearted smile, Philip mumbled, "Don't be so sure."

He walked to the front of the auditorium as stiff as a board. "Folks, I'm not feeling very well this evening so I apologize if this message doesn't come out right. I don't know if it's just nerves or what, but I'm really struggling—"

Brother Michaels stood up. "Church, you heard the brother! He needs our prayers. Let's go ahead and pray for the preacher before he gets into his message."

Somehow, that didn't make Philip feel any better. Even so, it gave him just enough time to get his breathing under control. As difficult as it was, he managed to preach his entire sermon without falling to pieces.

23

Carlos looked down at the blank sheet of notebook paper in front of him. Knowing what to write was extremely difficult. Mr. Bones expected him to tell on himself. They had already been over all of it anyway. He had already admitted his faults. Already apologized. Wasn't that enough?

He wrote "Dear, Mr. Bones."

Well, that was a beginning anyway. Now what? He replayed the event in his mind. "I'm writing this letter because you told me I have to. So, the other day I did something terrible."

Carlos put his pencil down. It wasn't exactly terrible. That was a bit too strong of a word. And if he included the fact that he was writing it because Mr. Bones told him to, that would sound babyish. No good! He balled the paper up into a wad and started over again with a fresh sheet.

He hated this letter idea. It wasn't like he ever really wanted to write it anyway. He didn't even want his probation officer to teach him. But Pop pretty much left him no choice. He had to pretend he still wanted to be homeschooled or he was going to receive an or-else that he didn't want to receive.

It took some trial and error, but eventually, the boy had a decent letter written out — one he fully expected Mr. Bones to find acceptable. He slid it under his pillow and laid his head down.

Carlos couldn't help but wonder how things were going to go once Mr. Bones arrived. The guy obviously had a right to be angry. Even if he wasn't, things between the two of them were going to be somewhat awkward. There was no way of getting around that.

Perhaps he could use a touch of humor to smooth ruffled feathers. Yes, laughter might just work. But what could he do that would make Mr. Bones laugh? Hmm...

He could always make the man his own superhero costume. Carlos chuckled as he pictured his probation officer's face. Now that he thought of it, Mr. Bones might take that the wrong way.

He needed a better plan — something that would make him laugh but nothing anyone could possibly consider inappropriate. Perhaps he could draw him a funny picture. Or come up with a string of jokes, puns, or riddles.

The only problem with humor was that Mr. Bones might see it the wrong way. He might think Carlos hadn't learned his lesson. If that were the case, his grounding sentence would probably be extended indefinitely. He did not want to go there.

Ma walked in with a bowl of tomato soup and a grilled cheese sandwich. "Ready for lunch?" she asked.

"Sure," Carlos told her.

After handing him his lunch, Ma sat down next to him. "So, what have you been doing up here all morning?"

Carlos wasn't sure if she was joking or being serious. "What do you think I've been doing?"

Ma smiled. "Good point," she said. "Let me rephrase... What have you been thinking about?"

"Lots, but mostly about how to make things go better with Mr. Bones tonight."

"Sounds like a good train of thought to me. Have you come up with any good ideas?"

Carlos shook his head. "I wish I had. Do you have any?"

Ma placed her hand on his knee. "The best advice I can give you at this point is to be cooperative, Carlos. Whatever Mr. Bones tells you to do, do it with no questions asked. If he says not to do something, then please, by all means, don't do it. And no matter what, Carlos, don't be goofy. This is not the time to play practical jokes or pranks or to try to have a good time. The man's upset with you. Just sit down and do your work and everything will be fine."

What kind of advice was that? Carlos couldn't believe it. How did Ma know he was thinking of taking a humorous approach? Perhaps she knew him better than he thought she did. "Thanks, Ma," he said.

"No problem, bud. You know your pop and I love you, right?"

Carlos smiled, "If you don't, you guys lie a lot because you tell me pretty much every day."

Ma removed her hand from his knee. "Carlos, when people tell you they love you, they are actually expecting you to tell them you love them in return."

That didn't make a lick of sense. Carlos may have only been thirteen, but he knew love was a lot more than just a word people said trying to get someone else to say it back to them. If he was going to tell somebody he loved them, it was going to be because he wanted to say it; not because they said it first. "No, I guess I didn't realize that," he told her.

Ma said, "Well, now you know. So, let's try again. Carlos, I love you."

"I know, Ma. You just told me a few minutes ago."

Ma stood to her feet. "Enjoy your lunch, Carlos. Pop will come up and check on you in a little while."

24

For once, Carlos was excited to hear his probation officer's voice. Doing school would be a welcome treat after seventy-two hours of complete and total boredom. Sitting up on his mattress, he rested his back against the wall and attempted to wait patiently.

Eventually Mr. Bones and Pop entered the room together. "Your Pop's going to sit over here and read a book while you and I get down to business."

"He doesn't have to stay in here," Carlos said. "I won't make up anything else about you."

"He has to stay. I cannot and will not be alone with you, Carlos. You have broken that trust."

The words were painful to hear, but Carlos understood where he was coming from. He had made a foolish decision, and there was no way to erase the damage that had already been done.

Mr. Bones handed Carlos his math book. "So, we were going to start on this the other day. Do you remember?"

"Yes, sir."

"Do you also remember the assignment I gave you?"

"We didn't get to an assignment."

"When we spoke on the phone, I told you to—"

"Oh," Carlos giggled. "This assignment." He reached under his pillow and pulled out a sheet of paper.

Mr. Bones took it and read over it thoughtfully. "This is a pretty good rough draft," he said after a few moments of silence.

Carlos was insulted. He had taken his time on that letter. He had his ma and pop sign it just like he was told to. No compliments for a job well done. Nothing but criticism. He hoped he had simply misunderstood. "A rough draft? What do you mean?"

"Well, looking this over, I now realize English is a weak spot for you, Carlos. You have so many misspelled words and misused punctuation marks that it makes your writing difficult to read. I'm going to go through here and circle all of the errors I see. When I'm finished, you're going to rewrite the paper — and this time in your neatest handwriting."

Carlos changed his mind. He would rather be sitting there in an empty room all by himself than having to rewrite that entire paper. It had taken him twenty minutes to write it. And for what? Just to do it all over again? He knew better than to share his opinion on the matter. "So, do you want me to do that for homework since we never got into our regular books the other day?"

Mr. Bones shook his head. "No, bud. I believe this is more important. Not only can we use it to improve your writing skills, but the more time you spend on this, the more you're going to understand how wrong it is to exercise such a lack of integrity."

"Pop, do you hear this?" Carlos asked.

Pop nodded.

"You always tell me we should leave the past in the past. You don't agree with Mr. Bones, do you?"

Mr. Bones didn't give Pop a chance to respond. "Carlos, your parents and I are on the same team. You are not going to turn us against each other."

"You're not my pop," Carlos insisted. "Pop, do you think this is right?"

Pop stood up. "Carlos, your probation officer is your teacher. You will do what he tells you."

Carlos wanted to bury his head in the sand. It was going to be a long evening. Why had he gone along with Pop's plan and apologized to Mr. Bones? All that did was bring more suffering into his life.

Mr. Bones didn't leave the house until it was time for Carlos to get ready for bed. He couldn't wait to see the man leave. As a matter of fact, leaving didn't sound like too bad of a plan. Perhaps he could show the probation officer what it felt like to be treated so harshly.

Slipping down the hall while Mr. Bones was talking to Pop and Ma, he made his way out the back door without being noticed. After closing the door behind him ever-so-quietly, he cautiously made his way to his probation officer's car. Seeing the driver's window down, he was certain the doors were unlocked.

Nope! For whatever reason, Mr. Bones had locked the doors. Like that would keep anyone from getting in!

Carlos climbed through the window and balled himself up in the floorboard behind the driver's seat. Mr. Bones had a sports jacket sitting on the back seat. Carlos pulled it over himself, hoping Mr. Bones wouldn't notice.

Five minutes later, the footsteps of his probation officer could be heard coming down the driveway. Carlos nearly

123

stopped breathing as the man fumbled with his keys. Fortunately, Mr. Bones didn't notice him. He started up the car and drove to his house.

After shutting off the car, Mr. Bones felt behind him and grabbed the sports coat. He pulled it right off of Carlos without even noticing he was there. It was a close call, but Carlos was winning. It was just about time to put his plan into action.

As the probation officer got out, he locked the doors with his keyless entry remote. The scheming teen slowly raised up and peeked his head over the back seat where he could watch Mr. Bones enter the house.

Once the man was out of sight, Carlos grabbed the door handle and opened it as quietly as possible. HONK! HONK! HONK! The lights began flashing. Why hadn't the thirteen-year-old realized opening the door from the inside would set off the alarm?

Leaping out of the car, Carlos ran around to the side of the house. A moment later, the alarm shut off without his probation officer even taking the time to walk around and check things out.

Carlos cupped his hands around his eyes and tried to peer through a window. Unfortunately, the shades were closed; he couldn't see anything. As he went from window to window, he found it impossible to see inside. He had no choice; if he was going to cause problems, he would have to find a way inside.

Tip-toeing up to the front door, Carlos tried the knob — it was locked. So were all of the windows and the back door. Unless he broke in, there was only one more option. There was a door he hadn't tried — it appeared to lead into the basement.

Carlos wasn't typically the kind of young man who enjoyed entering dark basements, but he was willing to make an exception. He cautiously descended the stairs. As he approached the door, he had no doubt he could get in — it wasn't even closed tight.

Scared stiff, Carlos made his way into the lowest level of his probation officer's house. He wanted to spy on the man or at least dig up some dirt on him. Somehow, he needed to show Mr. Perfect that he wasn't quite so perfect after all.

Finding a light switch along the wall, Carlos flipped it on. The basement looked like it was never used. It contained some old exercise equipment, boxes of old magazines, and dozens of cobwebs. Other than that, there wasn't much to look at. Regardless, Carlos left the light on as he crept up the stairs toward the main house.

When he got to the door, he nearly froze in his tracks. He had no idea where the door came out. For all he knew, Mr. Bones could be standing right in front of it. He put his ear to the door and listened intently — to nothing but silence.

He touched the knob — as he did, the telephone rang, and Carlos jumped back so quickly he stumbled all the way down the stairs, screaming as he fell. By the time he hit bottom, he was sore all over and was far too stunned to move. The door he had just touched flung open.

"Carlos?" Mr. Bones rushed down the stairs. "Are you okay? Wait a minute! What are you doing here?"

25

Mr. Bones had been in some pretty sticky situations before, but phoning Mr. Estrada was not going to be easy. The last time he was at their house, Carlos had accused him of wanting a free peep show; now this.

"Hi... um, Mr. Estrada? This is Philip Bones. We have a problem."

"What's that?"

"I heard a lot of commotion coming from my basement. When I went to check it out, I found your son laying in the floor at the bottom of my steps. Apparently, he sneaked into my car so he could break into my house once we arrived here. Then, somehow, he lost his footing on the stairs and tumbled all the way to the bottom."

Mr. Estrada was speechless.

"Sir, are you still there?"

"I am... I just don't know what to make of this... Is Carlos okay?"

Mr. Bones eyed the boy from head to toe again. "He's got some bruises and scrapes, but I believe he's fine. I'm going to bring him back to your place. If you want to take him in for an examination, you can, but I personally don't feel it's necessary."

"Okay," Mr. Estrada said before taking a deep breath. "I'll see you when you get here."

Mr. Bones hung up the phone and pointed toward the front door. "March," he ordered.

Carlos looked at his feet as he shuffled his way out of the house. "I'm sorry," he said.

"We'll discuss this when we get to your house. For now, I would prefer you keep your mouth closed."

"Yes, sir."

The ride to the Estrada residence was anything but pleasant. Mr. Bones feared Carlos was going to end up in serious trouble. His approach wasn't working. The boy was plainly not getting it.

Mr. Bones glanced in the rearview mirror at the young home invader. His face did not offer a hint of remorse. It was more a look of, "How can I get myself out of trouble for this one?" Either that or perhaps he was already planning his next move. Either way, Mr. Bones wasn't happy about it.

When they got to the house, they found Mr. Estrada waiting outside with a scowl on his face. He walked toward the car and wasted no time in opening the back door. "Carlos, Carlos, Carlos! What has gotten into you, my boy?"

"I'm sorry, Pop. Really, I—"

"Mr. Bones, it's time," Mr. Estrada growled. "My wife and I don't feel it's going to benefit Carlos to continue staying here. He needs more than we have to offer."

Mr. Bones wasn't about to argue with the man. It was becoming more and more obvious — Carlos needed a higher level of intervention. "I've been thinking along the same lines," he said. "Why don't we go inside and see if we can come up with a plan?"

"Sounds good," Mr. Estrada said, traipsing toward the house.

Inside, they all joined Mrs. Estrada in the living room. She had tears flowing down her face. "We've tried everything," she said. "Mr. Bones, what can we do?"

"At this point, it's obvious probation is not working," Mr. Bones said. "I could press charges on him for breaking and entering—"

"I didn't break in... the door was already open and—"

Pop wasn't having it. "Carlos, you went into another man's house without his permission. You have zero say-so in what happens from this point going forward. You can either sit here biting your tongue or you can go to your room and wait until a decision is made."

Carlos crossed his arms without uttering a word.

"As I was saying," Mr. Bones continued. "If I call the police, I can press charges on him for breaking and entering. We could also talk to your neighbor — the one he was spying on with the binoculars and see if they are also willing to press charges. That would guarantee him a spot behind bars for a minimum of one year."

Mrs. Estrada's crying intensified. "Do you think that's the best way?"

Mr. Bones felt sorry for her. He had seen plenty of Momma Bears break down in tears. Sometimes when they had to send their children away. Sometimes when judges ordered them to be locked up. And sometimes over the casket of the child they had brought into this world. He wished he knew the perfect solution. The answer that would guarantee Carlos would do an about-face and make positive changes in his life. But there were no guarantees he could make. "I don't know, ma'am," he said. "I'm just throwing ideas out there. Speaking of which, we could try to have him admitted to a psychiatric hospital. But most of them in the area are so full... it could be several months before he could get admitted."

"Are there any other options?" Mr. Estrada asked.

"Only one that comes to mind. We could try to find a residential placement. With his issues, it would need to be one that is only for boys – preferably either a boys' ranch, a military academy, or some type of a reform school."

Mr. and Mrs. Estrada looked at each other. "That's what we talked about before," Mrs. Estrada said. "I prefer that option."

"Me too," Mr. Estrada agreed.

"Okay," the probation officer said. "I will speak with Judge Williams and see if he will sign off on such a move. In the meantime, you folks will need to try to locate a facility you're comfortable with. Call around and see who has openings. Let me know when you've found one you like and we'll go from there."

"I don't even know where to start," Mr. Estrada told him. "Do you have any recommendations?"

Mr. Bones had to watch himself. If he made the wrong decision or recommended the wrong placement and something went afoul, the weight would rest on his shoulders. It would be much better if the parents made a decision themselves. A decision he didn't cram down their throats. "Just go online and start doing your research. There are plenty of options out there."

Mr. Bones knew the judge would go along with whatever decision he made, but it didn't make things any easier. Even though Carlos was a difficult young man to work with, he felt as though he was giving up on him. Why did tough love have to be so difficult?

The thirteen-year-old's eyes still showed no remorse, but they were filling with heartbreak. It was obvious he didn't want to be sent away, but his actions had screamed much louder than any words he could have spoken. The right choice had been made, whether the boy understood it or not.

"Carlos, I'm going to be leaving here in a minute. Do you have anything you would like your parents or me to take into consideration while we're looking into placement options?"

Carlos nodded, "I doubt you'll believe me, but I know what I did was wrong and I would be willing to do anything to make it up to you. I'll wash all of your windows, clean your car, do extra school work, let you take the mattress out of my room... anything! Please don't make me go to some ranch or military academy. I'll change. I just need more time."

Mr. Bones wished with everything in him that the boy was telling the truth. He knew better — the kid was sorry he got caught. He didn't want to suffer the consequences for his actions. End of story. "Carlos, buddy," he said, "as much as I hate to say this, you're absolutely right. I don't believe you. You're very good at manipulating people and telling them what they want to hear. I would be doing you a severe injustice not to take this next step."

Carlos shook his head, "So, there was really no point in me saying anything at all then, right?"

"There was a point, Carlos. I was hoping to see some tears stream down your face. To see that you genuinely regret your actions. But I'm not seeing that." Mr. Bones turned to Mr. and Mrs. Estrada. "Am I mistaken? Do you see anything on your son's face that tells you he's truly sorry?"

Both of the Estrada's shook their heads. "I'm afraid not," Pop said.

26

By the time Sunday morning rolled around, Philip was more than excited to begin teaching his teen class at Clover Baptist. Whistling "Jesus Loves Me," he entered the building and eagerly made his way down the center aisle, headed toward his normal pew — but someone was occupying his spot. Looking at her closer, he could hardly believe his eyes. "Kelly?" he asked.

"Philip... Fancy seeing you here."

"I don't know why you're surprised. This is my church."

"Your church? I've been coming here for over a month now. I've never seen you here."

That was a bit awkward. Kelly was his client's pediatrician, his secretary's niece, and now a member of his church who just happened to be sitting in his usual spot? "That's because I've been filling the pulpit for another church who was waiting for a new pastor," he said. "Wait a minute... you're not the new church member who's going to start teaching the girls' teen class?"

"I'm the one and the same."

Philip chuckled. What a small world!

"How's your little buddy doing? What was his name? Carlos?"

"It is. Carlos is doing… well, I guess I can't really discuss it due to confidentiality purposes."

"I understand," Kelly said. "Would you like me to start praying for him?"

What a sweet girl! Philip had no doubt she was offering more than lip-service. Prayer could certainly influence the situation. "That would be much appreciated," he said. "So how about you?... How are things at work?"

Kelly smiled. "I love my job! I am so thankful God directed my steps to become a pediatrician."

That feeling that came over Philip when he was speaking with Lisa suddenly came over him again. What was going on? He couldn't be attracted to two girls at the same time. He wasn't that kind of a guy. Whatever it was, he had to shake it. Small-talk was okay, flirting was not. "He's a wonderful God, isn't He?"

"You know it," Kelly replied.

Before they got too deep into their conversation, Pastor Jahmal came over to introduce them. "Looks like you guys have already met."

"That we have," Kelly smiled.

"I hope you two will work well together. The teen department is blessed to have you."

"Wait," Kelly said. "You're the other teacher? You didn't tell me that."

Philip smiled, "Oh, I guess I didn't. Sorry about that. I guess I should go ahead and take my seat. Looks like the pastor's heading up front."

Philip sat on the row in front of her. He couldn't wait for the Sunday School hour to take off. His lesson was certainly one the guys would enjoy. He had studied ten hours for a thirty-five-minute message.

After singing a couple of hymns, they were dismissed to their classes. Philip quickly made his way down the stairs and into his room. Moments later, a dozen teenage boys started piling in. "Good morning, gentlemen," he said.

"Morning," they all said in unison.

"Guys, I like to start things off with prayer. Which one of you would be willing to ask God's blessing on our class time?"

The room was silent. None of the boys even made eye contact with him. "Don't everybody volunteer at once now," Philip said.

Still getting no response, the new youth leader called on one of the boys he knew. "Dustin, you pray this week, and I'll call on somebody else next week."

"Do I have to?"

"Yes, you do. Everybody bow your heads," Philip said.

Dustin gave the man a dirty look before bowing his head and saying, "God, please bless this class time. Amen."

Philip was not impressed. It was God's house. Teenagers or not, they were all there for one purpose — to serve the Lord. The attitude was not necessary. "Guys, you're making this very difficult for me this morning. What's the deal here?"

A boy Philip recognized but didn't know spoke up, "Was this your idea, man? To take us away from the girls?"

Philip shook his head, "I see what this is about... No, guys, I had nothing to do with that decision. Pastor Jahmal decided to split the teen department up because he prefers smaller class sizes. All I did was agree to teach."

"So, what happens if you quit?"

Philip chuckled, "I'm not a quitter, gentlemen. But if God would call me to do something else, I'm sure He would supply you with a different teacher. But Pastor Jahmal is in charge of the church. If he wants there to be a boys' class and a girls' class, that's the way things are going to be. Now let's open up our Bibles. Shall we?"

The guys complied, but Philip had trouble teaching with any enthusiasm whatsoever. All of the excitement he had about teaching them had drifted out the window. By the time class was over, he felt like pounding his head against a brick wall. Perhaps he should have spent less time on studying and more time in prayer. He would certainly do things differently in preparing for the following week's lesson. Surely things would get easier in time.

Kelly was coming out of her class just as Philip left his. She was beaming. "How did things go?" she asked.

"Not so well," Philip admitted. "How about for you?"

"The girls were great! They were all engaged in the lesson. I believe every last one of them got something out of it... What happened in yours?"

Philip chuckled nervously. If he told her how things went, it could possibly bring about two completely different outcomes. Number one, Kelly could have a sympathetic ear. Feeling sorry for him, she might draw closer to him and could possibly begin a relationship. Number two, Kelly could think he was too immature to teach. If he couldn't handle a bunch of teenagers, how would he ever be able to lead a family?

After a few seconds of thought, Philip decided to tell her. If she was an option two kind of girl, it would make it easier for him. He would have no doubt they weren't meant to be together. It was time to put her to the test. "The guys were being somewhat rebellious. They're upset because they still want to be with the girls."

Kelly grinned, "That's guys for you."

"Hey, I resemble that remark," Philip laughed.

"You know it's true."

"If anybody knows, I do," Philip said.

As they approached the auditorium, Kelly encouraged Philip by telling him about some of the difficult youth groups she had worked with. She said no matter how difficult a group was, it was always possible to reach them. She promised to pray fervently for God's intervention.

Philip appreciated Kelly's uplifting spirit and agreed with her that things would get better in time.

They took their seats just as the song leader approached the podium. As they rose to sing, Philip dropped his hymn book. Embarrassed, he picked it up and glanced back to see if Kelly had noticed. Sure enough, she was grinning. She began to sing while Philip flipped back through to find the right page. That's when he noticed her voice. Wow, could that girl sing!

27

Mr. Bones gritted his teeth. He refused to utter the words that were trying their best to dive off of his tongue. The teenage boy sitting in front of him was driving the man insane.

"I ain't gotta call nobody sir," Ralph was saying for the fifth time in ten minutes. "Don't know why you always gotta act like you're somebody high and mighty. You ain't no better than me. No better than anybody for that matter. It's time to get over yourself. What... you think you can get the judge to take me off of probation just cause I don't want to call you, sir? You got another thing comin', bubba, let me tell you."

Mr. Bones had not spoken a single word for quite some time. His ears were growing tired of the repetitive, frustrating lecture his fifteen-year-old client enjoyed giving him. Had it been his first run-in with Ralph, Mr. Bones would have cut him off mid-sentence and put him in his place. But Ralph was different. Mr. Bones had learned the kid needed time to vent. If he didn't get it, he would never listen to a word that was said to him.

"One of these days, you're gonna have to climb off of your high horse and come to realize you're just like everybody else. You hearin' me?"

Mr. Bones didn't answer.

"You hearin' me?" Ralph repeated.

The probation officer squirmed in his chair and pretended to just come out of a daze. "Oh, I'm sorry... I'm allowed to speak?"

"Well, it is your office," Ralph snapped.

"I'm glad you finally realize that, Ralph. We need to—"

"What you mean I *finally*—"

Mr. Bones raised his hand up, "No, Ralph! I listened quietly the entire time you were talking. I did not interrupt you even one time. Now, it's time for me to talk and for you to listen."

"But—"

Mr. Bones shook his head, "You've had your say. Zip it!"

Rose tapped on the door. "Philip, you have other clients waiting in the lobby. Are you about finished up in here?"

Mr. Bones looked at his watch. Ralph had already been in his office for an hour, and they hadn't gotten anywhere. "Sure, Rose. I'll be out in a moment."

Ralph smiled, "Guess that's it for today, huh?"

The fifteen-year-old heathen had done it again. He had gotten his way, and there was nothing the probation officer could do about it. "You're free to go," he grumbled.

Seconds after Ralph left the office, Billy came in. He pulled his pants up and took a seat. "Hey, Mr. B!"

"Billy, you know—"

"I know, Mr. Bones... I just had to say it."

Mr. Bones chuckled, "How have things been going, bud?"

"Not bad. I'm getting better. The other day I broke into this cop's garage and huffed some gas. He never even knew I was in there!"

"Billy, you know you shouldn't joke—"

"Who says I'm jokin'?"

Mr. Bones picked up the telephone, "Well, in that case, perhaps I'll just call the sheriff and you can tell him more about this."

"You got me, Mr. Bones. I was just messin' with ya."

Mr. Bones put the phone back down. He knew he could get the truth out of him. "That's what I thought. So seriously, how are things going, Billy?"

"I'm doing a lot better, Mr. Bones. Ain't been smokin' no weed, stealing nothin', skippin' school. I be doin' alright."

Mr. Bones smiled. The reports he was getting on Billy were much better than the ones he used to get. That boy was on the right track! "That's what I like to hear, bud," he said. "Since you're doing so well, I'm going to go ahead and mark your file that you checked in and send you on your way."

"That fast? Where's the real Mr. Bones?"

"The real Mr. Bones is running behind and has a lot on his plate today."

"No problem," Billy said. "I'll have to remember that the next time I have an appointment and I've got other things to do. See ya, Bones."

"Now you know—"

Pretending he didn't hear a word, Billy walked out of the office.

The probation officer jumped up from his chair and followed him. "Billy, it doesn't work that way, man."

"We'll see about that. If you can cut things short, so can I. Ain't sayin' I'm goin' to. Just sayin' I have the same rights as you."

"That's the Billy I remember," Mr. Bones chuckled. "Always have to be right."

"Hey, you know me. I ain't gonna make no bones about it."

Mr. Bones couldn't help but laugh. It had been a while since he had used that phrase. Somehow it had slipped his mind.

After rushing his way through a few more check-ins, he finally found the time to make the phone call he was dreading. "Mrs. Estrada, this is Mr. Bones. Is your husband available?"

"No, he's out right now."

"No problem. Do you have a minute?"

"Sure. What's up?"

"I spoke with the magistrate this morning, and he's on board with the idea of having Carlos admitted into a residential facility. Have you all had any luck finding a place with openings?"

"Hold on a second," Mrs. Estrada said. "Let me step outside."

Mr. Bones could hear her walking, but she didn't say another word until a door opened and closed behind her. "It's a struggle, Mr. Bones. The military academies are full. The residential places that specialize in helping teenagers overcome sexual-related offenses want anywhere from $5,000 to $8,000 per month; there's no way we can swing that. The group homes for boys and the ranches we've called won't consider taking him because they're fearful he might pose a danger to their other students — they claim the liability is too high. We feel like we're drowning here."

"Have you checked with your insurance company to see if they might be willing to pay for treatment options?"

"Yes," Mrs. Estrada sighed. "They will pay for certain types of programs. But they are extremely selective and there is so much red-tape involved that it would take months to get him anywhere. We can't wait that long."

Mr. Bones could hear the frustration in her voice. "Have you all given up?"

Mrs. Estrada grew silent for a moment before saying, "No. We're still trying. I'm just saying it's not looking very promising."

"Okay… I'll talk to some of my colleagues without revealing your son's identity; maybe someone can point us in the right direction. Something will give."

Just as Mr. Bones hung the phone up, Rose tapped on the door. "There's a young lady here to see you."

"Send her back," he replied.

Check-in day was always full of chaos. Mr. Bones quickly filed a few folders away while he awaited the grand entrance of his next client.

A moment later, a young lady appeared at his door — but she wasn't a client. It was none other than Lisa, the playdough artist herself. "Philip!" she exclaimed. "I missed hearing your good preaching at church yesterday. I just came by to see how things went with your new youth group?"

"Wow, Lisa! I didn't expect to see you here. I mean, I'm glad you stopped by—"

"But?"

"Today has just been crazy. I've had client after client coming in, and I just got off of a difficult phone call."

"That bad, huh?"

"I have a distraught family who's in desperate need of a residential placement for their son."

"I bet I know why God sent me over here," Lisa smiled.

"Why's that?"

"First, tell me about this kid. Don't tell me his name or anything, but what kind of placement's needed?"

"It's a difficult case. The family doesn't have a lot of money but their son is acting out sexually and needs a place where he can get help without posing a danger to others."

"What would I get out of the deal if I found the perfect placement for him?"

Philip chuckled, "Do you really think you can?"

"There's a good possibility. Hold on a sec and let me make a phone call."

"Sure," Philip said.

Lisa pulled out her cell phone and flipped through her contact list. A second later she had the phone up to her ear. "Hey Ryan, this is Lisa... I have a question for you. Would you all consider taking in a young man who has a history of acting out sexually?... I don't know... Would you mind speaking with a gentleman I have here with me? He could give you more information."

28

Carlos didn't want to admit it, but he was scared out of his mind. Ma said there was a possibility he would wind up in a juvenile detention center; they were running out of options.

The boy had already spent a month in juvie. He didn't want to experience that again. He begged Ma to give him another chance. "I understand why you guys are so upset... but I won't do it again," he pleaded.

Ma was unmoved. "You cannot live here until you get help," she said. "I love you, son. But enough is enough."

"I don't need help, Ma. I just made some mistakes. I'm not going to make them ever again."

Ma exited the room, shaking her head.

Carlos punched his mattress. He was sick and tired of being locked up in his private cell. He couldn't stand the fact that nobody would take his thoughts into consideration. Why should he continue staying in his room and trying to comply with their discipline? It wasn't going to change anything — that was obvious.

Carlos got off of his mattress and stormed out to the living room.

"What are you doing?" Ma yelled. "Get back in that room!"

Carlos shot her a dirty look and asked, "Why should I?"

"Carlos Antonio Estrada!" Ma raced across the floor and grabbed him by the ear. He should have seen that one coming. Ma forced him back into his room. Releasing his ear, she yelled, "Don't you ever speak to me that way! You get back on that mattress and don't move!"

Carlos got on the mattress and screamed, "This isn't fair! You hate me! So does Pop! I ought to just kill myself!"

Just as the last word flew from his mouth, the phone rang. "Don't move!" Ma demanded before making a mad dash for the phone.

The boy who had practically given up on life wasn't about to stay put. It wasn't like Ma was going to wrestle him back to his room while she was talking on the phone. He crept down the hall. Hiding around a corner, he eavesdropped on Ma's call.

"That's wonderful... I'll talk it over with my husband when he gets home... I'm sure he'll be on board with it... Yes, yes, thank you!"

Ma giggled with joy as she hung up. "What was that all about?" Carlos asked, popping around the corner.

Ma's radiant smile was replaced with fury. "Get back to that room!" she demanded.

Carlos didn't wait for his ear to be yanked on this time. He ran back to his room before he could be told a second time. Ma trailed close behind. "What has gotten into you today?" she yelled.

"I'm bored out of my mind in here!"

"Well, maybe you should have thought about that before you acted out... Anyway, that was your probation officer on the phone. It looks like he's found a placement for you."

Carlos was disappointed. His mom was ecstatic and giggling because she had found a place to ship him off to? What did that say about how much she loved him? "What kind of placement?"

"A young Christian couple has recently started a ministry for youths who have issues similar to yours. They just opened and in order to get the word out, they're going to allow their first five students to be enrolled free of charge."

"How many other kids are there?"

"That's just it, Carlos. They're brand new. So right now, you will have two adults to give you their undivided attention."

"You mean there are no other kids?"

"Exactly! It's perfect."

Carlos was glad she thought so. Two shrinks with no experience were going to pester the daylights out of him. Then again, he was sure he would at least have his freedoms restored. No more bare room to live in every second of every day!

29

The juvenile probation department's list of clients was ever increasing. It was time for another intake. Mr. Bones quickly perused the young man's file; he looked like a decent kid who had simply made one bad decision.

In the lobby, he saw a teen who definitely stood out compared to the others who found themselves under his supervision. "Dawson? I'm Mr. Bones."

The sharply-dressed seventeen-year-old rose to his feet and shook hands with his new probation officer. "Nice to meet you," he said.

"Dawson, I appreciate the fact that you dressed up for this appointment. That says a lot about your character."

Dawson grinned, "Actually, this is how I always dress, sir."

"Even better... Did your brother come with you?"

"He wanted to, but he had to work."

If first impressions meant anything, Dawson was going to be an easy client to work with. "No problem. Let's head back to my office so we can get better acquainted with one another."

"Would you like the door open or closed?" the boy asked.

"Close it if you don't mind."

"Sure."

Dawson sat down before Mr. Bones even told him he could.

"So, Dawson..." Mr. Bones said as he took out his pen and notepad. "Tell me why you're here today."

"Can I ask you a question first?"

"You may."

"How long do you expect this meeting to last?"

"Somewhere in the neighborhood of an hour."

"If you weren't meeting with me, what would you be doing?"

Mr. Bones wondered where this conversation was headed; he was having trouble reading the young man. "I don't really know. I run a pretty tight schedule – visiting schools, handling check-ins, making phone calls, attending court hearings... I'm a busy man."

"Well, I'll tell you what," Dawson said, pulling out his billfold. "I'm willing to make your day a bit easier. What if I give you one hundred bucks and we cut the meeting? You can just document my file and say we met – write down whatever you want about me; it'll be a done deal and we can both get on with our lives."

Mr. Bones hadn't seen that one coming. "Where did you get a hundred bucks?"

"A hundred bucks is pocket change, man. I can sweeten up the deal if it's not enough for you. How much you need?"

Mr. Bones couldn't believe his ears. "Put that money away, Dawson. Never, I mean never, try to buy your way out of trouble. That will only get you buried so deep you'll never be able to find your way out."

Dawson pulled more money out of his billfold and reached it out toward Mr. Bones. "I'm not the kind that's going to rat you out, man. Don't think of it as a bribe. Think of it as a business transaction. Three-hundred; that's my final offer."

Mr. Bones pushed his hand away. "No, Dawson. Put the money back in your pocket and tell me why you're here."

Mr. Moneybags set the cash on his lap. "Alright, if you want to waste all of your time with me, we can do that."

The probation officer was slightly amused. To the best of his recollection, that was the first time a juvenile had attempted to bribe his way out of a meeting with him. If he wasn't a man of moral principle, he might have considered taking the kid up on the offer. But that wasn't him. He could never stoop that low. "That's exactly what I want, Dawson," he said. "What got you in legal trouble?"

The teen smiled, "My neighbor turned an ant hill into a volcano, man. She got all upset with me because I paid a guy to board up her windows."

"Why would you do something like that?"

"You'd have to live there to understand. The old lady's always staring out her window, watching our every move, man. We get tired of it."

"So, the lady found out you were behind it and called the police?"

"She did. Crazy, huh?"

"Oh, I'd say," Mr. Bones agreed, realizing Dawson was going to be more work than he initially suspected.

Their meeting lasted well over an hour. Mr. Bones would have continued grilling him longer, but he had an appointment at the Estradas' place. "I need to see you again next week," Mr. Bones told him. "It shouldn't take as long next time, but allow yourself at least twenty minutes."

"No problem," Dawson said. "But I'll bring my greenbacks in case you change your mind and want to free up some time on your schedule."

"That's not going to happen, bud. But get out of here; keep yourself out of trouble."

"Will do. Nice meeting you, man."

Mr. Bones chuckled to himself as his new client left the office. That kid had a warped sense of reality if he had ever seen one. Before his next meeting, he would have to develop a plan for reforming Dawson's way of thinking.

After a rush-job of organizing his office, Mr. Bones told Rose he had to head out. "I doubt I will be back before we close," he told her.

"I understand. See you in the morning," Rose replied.

Mr. Bones was not looking forward to his visit with the Estradas. It made him feel like a failure. After all of the time and effort he had poured into Carlos, he hated that it had come down to this. But he knew there were clients he couldn't reach alone. Carlos needed additional involvement.

When the probation officer got to the house, he found Mr. Estrada pacing back and forth in the yard. "We're doing the right thing, aren't we, Mr. Bones?" he asked.

"Yes, sir," the probation officer replied. "I know it's difficult, but I'm proud of you and your wife for taking this stand. I support you one-hundred percent... How is Carlos taking the news?"

"He's telling us we're horrible people. Says this young couple has no proven track record and for all we know, they could be abusive—"

"I've already received a criminal background check on them," Mr. Bones said. "They have no record whatsoever. Even though Carlos will be in a residential placement, I will be communicating with him on a regular basis. He'll be fine."

"I know, I know," Mr. Estrada said. "I'm just telling you what Carlos is saying."

"Gotcha... Do you mind if I go in and speak with him for a minute?"

"Sure. I'm going to stay out here though. I need the fresh air."

"Understood," Mr. Bones said before walking to the door and knocking.

A moment later, the teary-eyed Mrs. Estrada answered. "This is so hard," she said.

"I know," Mr. Bones told her. "But in the end, it will be worth the heartache. Is Carlos in his room?"

"He is. You can go in and speak with him if you'd like."

"Thank you," Mr. Bones said.

He didn't know how the teenager was going to respond to seeing him, but he had to check in with him one last time before he moved away.

He tapped on the door frame as he entered the room. "Hey, Carlos," he said as he walked in.

"Aren't you forgetting something?" the boy asked.

"I don't believe so."

"You're by yourself. Did you forget you're afraid to be alone with me?"

"There's an exception to every rule, bud... How do you feel about the placement you're heading to?"

"Do you want me to be honest?"

"Of course."

Carlos put a smug look on his face. "I'm excited about going. It will be good for me to get out of this house for a while and not to have you coming by and trying to tell my parents how to raise me."

Mr. Bones saw right through that charade, but he decided to go with the flow. "Awesome, man. I'm glad you have such an optimistic outlook on this thing. As long as you go with the right heart, you'll come back a better person for it."

The probation officer hoped the boy's heart would change while he was away. He had seen many young people fall through the cracks because they refused to change no matter how many opportunities they were given. Only time would tell.

In the meantime, he couldn't help but wonder what he was going to do with all of the free time he was going to have — then again, he knew from past experience that something or more likely someone would move into that slot before he even knew what happened.

Seventeen-year-old Dawson is going to require a lot of one-on-one attention. Will it even be possible for Mr. Bones to snap him back to reality? Be sure to read *Reforming Dawson* to find out.

Note from the author: If you enjoyed this book, please let me know by leaving a review at your favorite online book retailer!